About

Scott Hunter was born in Rc   ___ ..us
educated at Douai School in Woolhampton, Berkshire. His
writing career began after he won first prize in the Sunday
Express short story competition in 1996. He currently
combines writing with a parallel career as a semi-
professional drummer. He lives in Berkshire with his wife
and an elderly Cocker Spaniel called Archie.

The Fragile Cage

Scott Hunter

Acknowledgements

Thanks to Stuart Bache (Books Covered) for the cover design, to my man on the inside (he knows who he is), and to my insightful and excellent editor, Louise Maskill

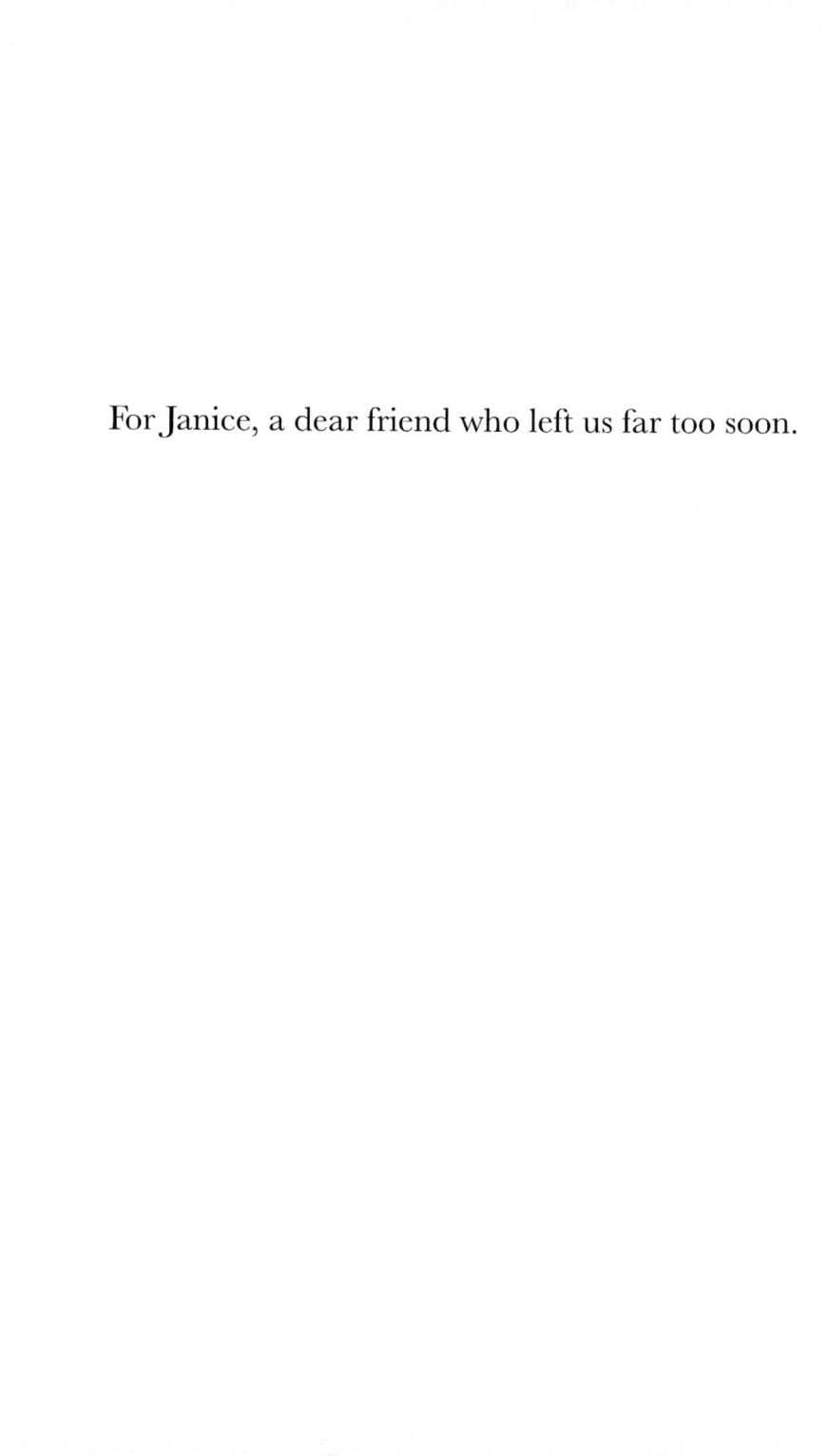

For Janice, a dear friend who left us far too soon.

'We are all just a car crash, a diagnosis, an unexpected phone call, a new found love or a broken heart away from becoming a completely different person. How beautifully fragile are we...'
--Samuel Decker Thompson

Author's Note

1968 was a long time ago. Things were changing faster than we realised at the time. The Beatles had rearranged the face of popular music, and with Sgt. Pepper they kick-started a great awakening of musical experimentation. '68 saw many notable releases: The White Album, Cream's Wheels of Fire, Hendrix' Electric Ladyland, Floyd's A Saucerful of Secrets to name a few. In America, the war in Vietnam had given rise to a new generation looking for a fairer and more peaceful political landscape. The movement reached a peak at Max Yasgur's farm in '69, where three days of love, peace and music marked both the zenith and the beginning of the end of the flower power culture.

I, as a twelve-year-old boy, knew nothing of this; I was preparing for my first experience of an English boarding school where the teachers were (without exception) a bunch of maverick characters, any of whom would sit very well within the pages of an Evelyn Waugh novel. Nonetheless, apart from this disturbing incarceration, my memories of the sixties are largely happy. Here in the UK, policemen could still be trusted, our parents didn't have to fret about where we were during the holidays, telephone boxes still worked with buttons A and B and a few coins. Cars were characterful and very British in appearance – between 1966 and 1969 my father owned a Ford Anglia, an Austin A40 and (my personal favourite) a lime green Cortina Estate with bench seats and no safety belts. Cheery forecourt attendants would fill up your tank (with or without a tiger), and call you *sir* or *madam*. There were no stringent Health and Safety rules and regulations, nor was there very much political correctness in evidence.

Perhaps I'm viewing the past through rose-tinted spectacles, but looking back, it seems to me that we lived in a more wholesome age, enjoyed a more innocent way of life and, for the most part, were much richer for it. Has the world improved? Has the communications revolution made our lives any better? Political correctness? The new Woke culture? I'm not sure that it has. Well, I'm digressing to a much larger extent than usual so I'll leave it there. The world of 1968 is long gone, but this is the world I invite you to revisit, or perhaps visit for the first time if you're not quite as long in the tooth as the author. Whatever 1968 was to you, this is Cameron Kyle's world, and he has to deal with it (as well as a lot of other stuff). I hope you enjoy meeting him.

SH, October 2022

Prologue

The warehouse was dim and dingy, yellow fluorescent tubes casting puddles of grubby light on the unfinished concrete floor. Racks of automotive spares filled the main body of the room, stretching to the ceiling like Meccano prototypes for some ambitious home engineering project. Rain rattled thunderously on the warehouse roof and here and there puddles of oily water were topped up by a constant dripping from untended cracks and holes lurking in the shadows above.

Three men were gathered in the kitchen area beneath a single unadorned bulb, smoking and drinking tea. A skein of spider web stretched from the bulb to a corner of the mezzanine roof beneath which they were huddled. None of the men looked happy; their faces were pinched and gaunt, the conversation sporadic and laced with tension.

'Said 'e'd be 'ere by now,' one said, drawing on an almost spent cigarette.

'Always drags 'is feet come payday,' another man with thick, greying hair nodded. 'We take the risks, 'e gets the cream.'

'Don't let 'im 'ear you say that,' the first man hissed, tucking the extinguished butt behind one ear. ''E'll kill you soon as look at you.'

'Bring back the old days, that's what I say,' the third man

offered. 'Ken might've been a lot of things, but 'e never let us down, did 'e?'

'Never,' the first agreed.

'*And* he spoke the same lingo,' the second pointed out. 'This fella, well, they think different don't they, these continentals?'

There was a chorus of assent. More cigarettes were found and lit. The rain continued its constant battering.

'How long shall we give 'im, then?' the man with the thick grey hair asked.

'Long as it takes,' the first man said. 'You know what 'e's like about order.' He drew long and hard on his Player's No. 6. 'And don't forget what 'appened to young Michael, neither.'

Heads were shaken as the incident was recalled.

'Didn't deserve that, not in my book,' the second man said. 'Got to give at least one second chance, right?'

'Know what I heard Saturday night?' The grey-haired man looked at his colleagues. 'You mightn't believe it, but I reckon there's a grain of truth.'

'Go on, what?' The first man blew smoke. 'I could do with some good news.'

'Harry Worthington comes to me, and 'e says, I've heard that Ken's planning an early exit.'

'Harry Worthington? You can't trust a bloody word that bloke says.' The first man shook his head bitterly. 'Told me to bet on some knackered old nag at Newbury last month. Come in last, didn't it?'

There was a brief burst of laughter.

The grey-haired man restored order with a raised finger. 'Serious, though. Harry reckoned he 'eard it from the 'orse's mouth.'

'Funny.' The first man gave a disparaging snort.

'No, serious,' grey-hair insisted. 'Harry knows one of the screws – dodgy geezer, they say, smuggles all sorts in and out if you cross 'is palm. Now, this bloke says Ken's up to somethin' for sure. Remember 'e was in solitary? Well, not any more. He's wangled his way out of that.'

'You can bet old Ken knows which palms to grease,' the third man said to another chorus of nods.

'Makes no odds, anyhow,' the first man said. 'Even if Ken walks right out of there, 'e can't just pick up the reins like before. 'E'll have to lie low for the rest of 'is life.'

'Like bloody Biggs.' The third man made a rude gesture and there was more laughter.

'Exactly,' the second man said. 'So we're stuck with the Italian, whether we like it or not.'

'*Stuck?*' A new voice spoke from the shadows, deep and clear with a pronounced and musical cadence. '*Stuck* is not a word I have heard used in this context. Would any of you gentlemen care to explain the usage and application for the benefit of this poor student of English?'

The mood had darkened in an instant. The grey-haired man had visibly paled, his cigarette hanging trembling from his lips as he grappled for a suitable answer.

'All tongue-tied, Mr Sayer? It is the correct idiom, yes?'

The new arrival stepped into the dim light of the single bulb. He was dressed in a long overcoat and wore a wide trilby that hid the expression in the dark sockets beneath its brim. The sight of an aquiline nose, full, subtly pigmented lips and a strong chin fresh from a razor's keen edge sucked at the group's composure as if they were panicking rabbits caught in a car's oncoming headlights.

'Figure of speech, boss,' the grey-haired man managed after another quick pull on his cigarette. 'Don't mean nothin' by it.'

'Of course, of course. I am having a little fun, that is all.' The Italian smiled, revealing a row of even, white teeth. 'May I join you?'

There was a brief scuffle as all three men attempted to offer their chairs.

The Italian raised his hand, went to the corner of the kitchenette and found a spare. He pulled it over, sat down and elegantly crossed one leg over the other. 'Now, to business.'

The tension dispersed. The second man wiped a tiara of perspiration from his forehead with a grimy pocket handkerchief.

The Italian looked at each man in turn. '*Cosi*. Last week was a fine success, gentlemen. Both clients have elected to offer the maximum ... premium, shall we say. Which of course means that we are able to apply an even split of the profits for each participant.'

Since the Italian's arrival the drumming on the rooftop had doubled in intensity; now gusts of wind were shaking the warehouse doors. The mood in the kitchenette, however, had reached a sunnier plateau. Broad smiles were exchanged.

The Italian reached into his overcoat pocket and produced two envelopes. The three men glanced at each other. With a broad smile the Italian distributed the envelopes, one to the first man and the other to the third man. The second, Sayer, looked confused.

The Italian spread his hands. '*Molto bene*,' he said to the two beneficiaries. 'You are free to go. Why do you stay?' He opened his hands palms up, adopting a quizzical expression.

The two made a hurried exit. The warehouse door roared as it was opened to the elements, then banged shut.

Sayer stood up warily, uncertain.

'Jack, isn't it?' The Italian was still smiling.

'Jack? Yeah … Jack Sayer.' He moistened his lips.

The Italian came closer, put an arm around Sayer's shoulders. 'Jack, you must know … I always strive to keep everyone happy.'

'Sure.' Sayer wanted to move, but he was backed up against the sink and the Italian's grip was firm.

'Since Ken was taken away, you know we have made good work together.'

'Yeah … I've no complaints.'

The Italian hugged him closer. 'No complaints! That is exactly right. We don't want any complaints, do we, Jack? We have to *deal* with complaints.'

Sayer could smell a hint of garlic on the man's breath. He swallowed. 'What I said earlier, I mean, it was nothing, I was just–' Sayer was aware that the Italian was doing something with his free hand. The man's mouth was pressed to his ear. He felt a sudden pressure, a stinging sensation in his chest, a probing sliver of pain that intensified until his breath caught in his throat and a warm wetness crept across his torso as though something hot had spilled and was burning his flesh. The Italian's mouth was still at his ear. The man was singing softly, the words making no sense.

… *It's bloomin' Italian…*

Sayer's thoughts tumbled on incoherently until his knees buckled and he realised he was lying face down on the floor.

He managed to roll, turn his head; the Italian was standing over him, a long, thin blade held loosely in his hand. He was still singing, but now in a louder, more strident voice.

As his eyelids grew heavier Sayer's final impression was that the Italian was waving his stiletto up and down and from side to side like a conductor directing his orchestra.

Sayer's heart ran out of blood to pump. It missed one beat, then two, then three, then stopped altogether, while the Italian synchronised the movements of the stiletto to perfection. With a final flourish, Sayer's life came to its climactic crescendo.

The Italian turned as if to face an invisible audience and bowed once, twice, three times, before walking into the darkness as silently as he had arrived.

Prologue Part Two

Cameron Kyle opened his eyes to a sensation of complete disorientation. He was lying flat on his back, the ceiling above him an unfamiliar rectangle of white plaster. He moved his right arm and found that he was attached to some foreign object by a length of tubing. The lighting was dim, subdued. His head ached with a fierce throbbing and his mouth was dry, his tongue clamped to the roof of his mouth like an overcooked slice of bacon.

He was vaguely aware of furtive, hushed movement, a whisper of terse instructions and then, as his olfactory senses kicked in, the sterile odour of medication combined with something baser, more metallic – a smell he recognised with a jolt of alarm as human blood. He tried to move his other arm and winced as a stab of pain travelled from his wrist to his elbow. He looked down at the offending limb to find it encased in plaster of Paris.

He lay back on the pillows, exhausted by his efforts. His mind, blank up to this point apart from an automatic recording of physical sensation, now began to rewind his memory's stored images, presenting them to his befuddled brain in non-sequential patterns that left him even more confused than at his moment of awakening.

There was a house, a run-down terraced property. It was after dark, mid-evening, perhaps. Traffic passing by on some arterial road nearby. Shapes moving behind curtains. Someone familiar, approaching the front door, knocking. He was by the window, just to the left as the door was opened. A flat report, like a muted clap of thunder, a shadow directly in front of him, an acrid, burning smell. Someone laughing, a cruel, jibing, humourless laugh incongruously morphing into a snatch of opera.

Someone lying at his feet, quite still. His own voice, shouting. He was on his knees, turning the prone body, his hands were on the torso, red hands, warm liquid trickling between his fingers. Somewhere in the background the sound of a siren wailing, drawing closer. The door a frame of lifeless yellow light, cigarette smoke drifting across the empty space like autumn fog. His own voice, yelling, cajoling, willing the still shape before him to respond.

More voices at the door, a whipcrack sound like a firework going off. An explosion of pain in his head. Darkness, a sensation of falling...

'Mr Kyle?' A female voice, kindly, soft, warm. 'It's good to have you back with us.'

He looked up at the woman by his bed, uncomprehending. A silver watch, was attached to her uniform; he concentrated on its components, followed the tracking of the second hand as it passed each neatly inscribed Roman numeral. Was there some similar mechanism that could explain his current circumstances? If the watchmaker's talent could create a device to track the passing seconds with such relentless precision, then surely his impaired memory could be recalibrated in similar fashion?

He tore his eyes from the timepiece and tried to focus on the woman's face, but the details of her features were

indistinct, like an underdeveloped photograph. He wanted to ask her to explain everything, but the only sounds he was able to coax from his throat were a series of guttural grunts.
'It's all right. Don't try to talk. Here, let me give you some water.'
Cool liquid filled his mouth, a cloth was passed across his lips. He closed his eyes. It was too hard to stay awake.
He slept.

Forty-eight hours later, Kyle's world had assumed a more understandable, albeit undesirable, clarity. Information came at him in small, bite-sized pieces as prescribed by Sister Mary, the ward sister. She had five children, her husband was a tax inspector and the family attended Mass religiously every Sunday. Her favourite flowers were roses. Such was Kyle's current knowledge of the woman tasked with his immediate rehabilitation.

He had been in Intensive Care for ten days before being transferred to a side ward, which was bare and functional. Someone had attempted to lighten the austere decor with flowers, loosely arranged in a heavy cut-glass vase. They sat on a small table by the window, a collection of orange and yellow blooms he couldn't identify, red carnations, a spray of greenery.

His arm was broken and his head was bandaged. A bullet had skimmed his forehead and his skull had suffered a colossal impact, hence the constant headache. There was apparently some question regarding shrapnel, a possible minor penetrative injury in or around the same area. His arm must have been damaged afterwards; that was the bit he couldn't remember. What he did remember, though, was that

Colin Slattery, his close friend and colleague, was dead, and that it was probably his fault.

Patterson was his first visitor. The blinds were, as per Kyle's request, fully drawn, and the Detective Inspector was informally dressed, leading Kyle to assume it must be a weekend or some time in the evening. He slept pretty much all the time, and his internal clock had stopped ticking. What did the time matter? Nothing much mattered any more.

He watched Patterson approach with his usual shifty glance to the right and left, a habit born from years of entering and searching suspicious premises.

'Hello Kyle.' Patterson sat on the visitor's chair, removed his hat, and placed it awkwardly on his lap. 'Good to see you making progress.'

Kyle nodded. Talking was still a huge effort.

'Sorry about DC Slattery. His family have been informed.'

There was no obvious response to this statement, so Kyle simply nodded again.

'You should have carried on with obs for longer. Bet it was Slattery's idea to go in.'

The events of that night were still a series of disconnected events in Kyle's mind, like carelessly scattered pieces of a child's jigsaw; they would take some time to assemble in the correct order. He raised his shoulder, a slight shrug.

'Be more assertive, that's what I've always told you. Did you try to talk him round?'

Kyle closed his eyes as fragmented snatches of conversation flicked through his mind. They'd been sitting in Colin's Cortina, a few doors along from the stakeout. They had a clear view, people coming and going at regular intervals; they were sure the main man – the big cheese, as

Colin called him – was present. Something big was going down. There'd be ample evidence to bring them in. Why not capitalise on the element of surprise?

'Well, did you?'

'I can't remember. Probably. Yes, we were supposed to be on obs only, I know that.'

It was Kyle's longest utterance since his injury, and it left him breathless.

'All right,' Patterson waved his hand. 'Take it easy. We don't want you doing yourself any further damage.'

Doing yourself. Kyle was alert enough to pick up on the implication: it *was* all his fault.

'Anyway, what's done is done. Our friends have taken flight. By the time we got to the property the place was empty.' Patterson held up his hands, palms outward. 'Shame you didn't take a stronger line. You know what Colin is like – *was* like. Sorry.'

'Is that how you see it?' Kyle tried to keep his breathing steady.

Patterson shrugged. 'Only partly, but it's the way you are, Kyle, isn't it? I've always said you need to show a little more backbone. You're a big fellow, a rugby player to boot, so you should have a lot more confidence than—'

'Go to hell, Patterson.'

Patterson was so surprised that his mouth fell open and his words dried up. It took him a moment to gather himself, during which his forehead creased into a frown. 'May I remind you who you're speaking to, DC Kyle? As your superior officer, I—'

'Maybe you didn't hear me,' Kyle said. 'I said *go to hell. Get out!*' He propped himself up on his good elbow. 'And you can take your sodding officious attitude with you while you're at it!'

'*What* is going on in here?'

Sister Mary had appeared in the doorway. She glared at Patterson. 'I said *quiet* conversation, five minutes only, and don't upset the patient. Please leave immediately.' She held the door open.

Patterson replaced his hat over his thinning hair and stood up. 'I'll overlook this, DC Kyle, as you're clearly still unwell.'

'I don't care what you do,' Kyle told him, 'and for your information it's *ex*-DC Kyle.'

'That's *enough*, Mr Kyle.' Sister Mary closed the door on Patterson's departing back. 'Now settle down. I'm turning visitors away for the next forty-eight hours.'

Kyle rested his head on the pillow as Sister Mary fussed around with efficient precision, updating his notes, refreshing his water, checking his medication. 'Mr Benjamin has his ward round tomorrow. He'll be able to answer any questions or concerns you might have.'

'Sister Mary?'

'Yes?'

'Remember to pray for me, won't you?'

She shot him a half-amused, half-disapproving look, picked up his tray of untouched food with a flourish, and left the room.

He was asleep again within minutes.

Mr Benjamin was a tall, ascetic-looking man in his late forties. Kyle had no preconceptions as to what a brain surgeon might look like but he supposed that Benjamin fitted the bill. His long, pale face loomed over Kyle's bedstead as he inspected Sister Mary's meticulously annotated charts. Several white-coated colleagues – registrars or senior housemen, Kyle assumed – hovered in the great man's wake, all looking terrified that Benjamin might fire some unanswerable question at the unluckiest of his entourage.

'So, Mr Kyle. A head injury, that's what we're all about today. Orthopaedics will be along tomorrow to talk about your arm. That's not my concern.' Benjamin pulled out an X-ray from a folder that Sister Mary, standing behind and to one side of the surgeon, had magically produced from a trolley just inside the door of the side ward. He held it up to the light and pursed his lips. 'Yes. A hairline crack in the frontal bone.' He lowered the X-ray. 'Which explains your hitherto slow pulse rate, high blood pressure and swollen optic disks – and those rather spectacular bruises beneath your eyes,' he added, almost as an afterthought. Kyle hadn't looked in a mirror since his admission, so he received the news of his panda-like appearance with an ambivalent movement of his head. 'The drip is a solution to draw water from your swollen brain, Mr Kyle, in case you were wondering. And the catheter a necessary evil for the time being, I'm afraid, to cope with the diuresis.'

'Your kidneys,' Sister Mary whispered from the rear by way of explanation. 'They're making too much urine at present.'

'*Thank* you, Sister,' Mr Benjamin gave a small bow of appreciation, followed by a withering glance towards his acolytes, a clear but unspoken suggestion that one of them should have offered this explanation rather than leaving it to the ward sister. 'Any questions, so far, Mr Kyle?'

Kyle felt the blood rising in his cheeks. 'Yes. When can I

get the hell out of here? Now would be good. Actually, *now* is too late.' Kyle made as if to get out of bed. He was suddenly furious that these people were conspiring to keep him imprisoned. He heard himself remonstrating with the medical team as though from a distance, paradoxically aware that this unexpected wave of stroppiness and aggression was wildly out of character. Sister Mary and a pretty young nurse he had first seen earlier in the day manhandled him back into bed.

When Kyle realised that he was unlikely to succeed in his unscheduled bid for freedom, he exhaled slowly and closed his eyes. 'Can you all just go away? I want to sleep.'

Benjamin's voice went on, apparently unfazed by the disturbance. 'Your agitation is to be expected, Mr Kyle. When your traumatised cerebral cortex has recovered and the swelling has reduced sufficiently, I'm sure you'll find yourself in a calmer state of mind. I'll see you again next week. There's an additional … problem we'll need to discuss, but I won't trouble you about it now.'

After Benjamin's departure, Sister Mary lingered behind. 'Really, Mr Kyle. There was no need for such a vulgar display.'

'Bugger off, Mary,' Kyle heard himself say. 'I'd like to be alone.'

He half-opened one eye to see Sister Mary trying her best to stifle a grin as she departed. One for the staff room coffee break, Kyle thought drowsily as he drifted off.

Days passed. Kyle woke up one morning to find a severe-looking woman in a tweed suit standing at the foot of his bed. 'Good morning, Mr Kyle. My name is Mrs Winder. I'm a psychologist. Mr Benjamin has asked me to have a word.'

Kyle groaned.

She pressed on, undeterred. 'I'm here to provide further explanation regarding your condition. You've experienced a severe trauma, Mr Kyle. The bullet struck your head directly over the right frontal cortex. You should know that the right cerebral hemisphere is the centre for critical reasoning.'

Kyle nodded slowly. 'Go on.'

Winder drew up a chair, placed her clipboard on her lap. 'This particular area of the brain is responsible for thought processes involved in the avoidance of risk. Your ... ah, your lack of inhibitions, general irritability, and occasional aggressive behaviour as reported by the senior ward sister are all directly attributable to your injury.'

'No kidding.'

Winder smiled thinly. 'I'm going to ask you some questions. This isn't a test, just answer as you see fit.'

Ten minutes later she told him that she had gathered sufficient information, and returned the paperwork to her briefcase.

Kyle was intrigued. 'Well?'

Winder took off her glasses and began to polish the lenses with a soft cloth. 'It's as I thought. The results suggest a high placement on something we call the psychopathic personality inventory.'

'What? So now I'm a psychopath?'

'Don't worry.' Winder gave him another tight smile. 'Most high achievers score pretty highly on the same index. Many successful people have psychopathic tendencies. It doesn't mean you're going to become the next Moors murderer.'

'*So* comforting. My mum will be delighted.'

Winder battled on. 'What I mean is that, although your higher neurological functions are thankfully still intact, your injury has caused a personality shift. It's very common with this kind of trauma.'

'So what does that mean exactly – in practical terms? Will it be permanent?'

She shook her head. 'It's hard to say. When the swelling reduces your cognitive functions may return to normal – or close to normal. When I say normal, I mean normal for you; we're all different. In practical terms … well, you'll probably be aware of an unusual disinhibition of behaviour. You might find yourself entering into situations, tackling problems and so on, in a bolder, dare I say more egotistical manner. You'll have to wait and see…' She tailed off.

'What?'

'I believe Mr Benjamin has … made you aware that the bullet sliver is located in an inoperable area of your brain.'

'Yes.' Kyle had been trying to bury that knowledge. He didn't want to be reminded of it.

Winder forced another smile. 'So there is a modicum of … unpredictability attached to your recovery. The swelling will reduce in time, as I've explained, but…'

'The fragment might kill me anyway.'

'We can't be sure, Mr Kyle, but let's be optimistic, shall we? Take it from me, that's by far the best way forward for you. Now, unless you have any further questions, we'll leave it there for the time being. I'll be back in a few days to see how you're getting on.'

'Yes, ma'am. Stiff upper lip and onwards into glory.'

Winder gave him a look that managed to combine clinical curiosity with a fair degree of sympathy. 'Just try not to let your potential for psychosis lead you into any challenging situations, Mr Kyle.' She nodded, collected her things and left him to his thoughts.

Kyle watched the hands of the wall clock slowly eat up the day. He had no idea what his future might look like, but according to Benjamin and Winder – reading between their carefully choreographed lines – it might be a short one. All he knew for sure was that he would not return to his role as a serving police officer. Patterson was right. Colin was dead and it was Kyle's fault. No one else could be blamed. He should have done something. *Anything.*

As he dozed, he imagined himself poring over a newspaper's *situations vacant* page. He scanned down the print until he came to a box advertisement which read:

Wanted: Psychopath. Immediate start. Good rates of pay. Full holiday entitlement and healthcare package. Apply with covering letter for immediate consideration.

Chapter One

Kyle groaned, stretched his arms. Time for the headache-severity calculation – the HSC. He rested his head on the pillow and went through the usual analysis. Today was somewhere less than ten, but above five. Maybe six point five-ish. Better than yesterday, which had been around eight to nine. He cautiously raised his head. The discomfort was bearable.

Today he'd be able to function, get some practical tasks done. He swung himself out of bed, planted his feet on the carpet. No double-vision. Another tick – it had taken a good six weeks for his eyesight to return to something close to normal.

Normal?

Nothing was normal anymore.

They'd discharged him three weeks after Winder's final assessment – twelve weeks after the incident. He'd dozed through Christmas and much of January, rejected Winder's advice to listen to the radio or chat to other patients, choosing instead to spend his time in sullen contemplation, watching the traffic crawl past on the busy London roads.

Now he was home.

And now the evenings were getting lighter. Spring was in the air and his first follow-up appointment with Benjamin was in four days.

Kyle got to his feet and took a few experimental steps. So far, so good. He made his way to the kitchen and took care to make use of his recently liberated arm as he filled the kettle, found the teapot and turned on the radio. Georgie Fame's Ballad of Bonnie and Clyde filled the room.

Bonnie and Clyde were pretty-looking people, but I can tell you, people, they were the Devil's children...

He flexed his arm as he waited for the kettle to boil. There didn't seem to be any loss of dexterity, and it was a relief to be free of the plaster.

'So, Colin old buddy, what do you suggest for today's agenda? A quick shuffle around Fine Fare, a walk in the park, another paperback?'

He had mixed feelings about many of Winder's suggestions, but especially this one. *Talk to Colin. Talk aloud. It'll help. Don't bottle it up. Let it out. Tell him how you're feeling. Chat to him. Trust me, you'll feel better for it.*

The hard part was the silence, but he was trying to work with it. He knew how Colin would respond as surely as he knew his own mind; they'd had an almost telepathic relationship. It had been a rare friendship, one that he felt privileged to have experienced. *Not everyone has a friend like that,* Winder had said. *Not everyone makes such a deep connection, so celebrate it. Remember the good times. Keep him alive in your memory.*

He warmed the teapot, dropped in two heaped teaspoons of PG Tips, then added the boiling water and left it to brew. He looked out onto the grey street. Rain was falling steadily, a few raincoat-clad bodies scurrying by, heads bent, dodging the puddles.

He grabbed a mug from the cupboard, fished a tea-strainer from the cutlery drawer and tried to place it over the mug but his hand was shaking so badly he almost dropped it. 'Why?' he yelled. 'Why, why WHY DID IT HAPPEN?'

He leaned on the sink, head swimming. *Try not to get worked up*, Benjamin's long, serious face loomed before him. *Your brain needs time to recuperate. Keep yourself in check.*

He took a steadying breath.

Come on, bud, Colin-in-his-head piped up. *Get yourself out. Do stuff. At least you've got the option.*

Kyle bit his bottom lip hard. 'Yep. Sure. You're right, as always.'

He changed quickly into jeans and jumper, shrugged on a jacket, grabbed his keys, threw the front door open.

And stopped.

'Rebecca?'

He was too surprised to say anything else. The girl who'd finished with him six months ago, the girl he'd have crossed fiery mountains for, was right here, in the flesh, on his doorstep.

'Hello, Cameron. I was wondering … well, how you are, you know?'

'How I am?'

'Yes. Got time for a cuppa? I'm buying.'

Better see what she wants, Colin said.

'Sure.' Kyle manufactured a smile. 'If you don't mind walking slowly.'

Chapter Two

'You're looking better.'

'Better than what, exactly?'

'Better than the last time I saw you.' Rebecca sipped her tea. 'You had so many tubes and stuff poking out of you I thought I'd wandered onto a *Dr Who* set.'

Kyle fiddled with his spoon. 'You came to the hospital?'

'Of course I did.' Rebecca's face softened. 'Why wouldn't I?'

'Visiting your ex?' Kyle said. 'The point being?' He instantly regretted his harsh tone.

Rebecca sighed. She was even prettier than he remembered. He couldn't hold her gaze, went back to spoon fiddling.

'We weren't working, Cam, you know that. We went over it – time and time again.'

'That much I do remember.'

She looked at him reproachfully.

'I miss you.' The words were out before he could stop them.

Rebecca reached across the table and placed her hand over his. 'Cam, we had a good time together. I don't regret any of it. But we have to move on, both of us.'

'You already have. My emotional progress has been held up a bit. How is Björn-the-lawyer, anyway?'

'His name is *Sven*, as you well know.' She smiled. 'He's fine. I'm happy. We both are.'

Kyle stirred his tea absently, clinked the spoon on the edge of his saucer. 'I'm glad for you,' he said. 'I really am.'

Rebecca withdrew her hand, sat back in her chair. He could still feel her touch on his skin; it lingered like a happy memory.

She looked him in the eye. 'I can't tell you how sorry I am about what happened … about Colin. It's too terrible. But you'll bounce back. You're still here, aren't you? You've been spared. There must be a reason for that.'

'Oh God, please don't invoke a higher power.'

'You just did.'

He shook his head, gave a humourless laugh. 'Ha ha. So I did. Well, well.'

She was silent for a moment. 'How bad is it?'

He looked away. 'It could be worse. My arm's healing. My brain might take a bit longer.'

'Cam, you could have been killed.'

He tapped the spoon on the tabletop. 'Sure.' He shrugged. 'But I wasn't. Colin was. Anyway, I'm fine. Really.'

'You always were a rubbish liar.'

He said nothing. They both knew she was right. He sipped his tea, which was slightly stewed. You couldn't get a decent brew these days unless you made it yourself. 'So, what do you want?'

'I told you. To see how you are.'

'Uh huh. Tick. And what else?' Two could play the "I know you" game.

Her eyelids dipped; her turn to inspect her cup. 'I was assigned a new case a few months ago.' She looked up. 'A tough one.'

'Oh yes?'

'Kenneth Munday.'

Kyle raised his eyebrows. "Tough" was underselling it. Munday was a violent lifer, inside for the murder of two child abusers and one wife-killer, the former two despatched while detained at Her Majesty's pleasure. He'd been deemed too volatile to mix with other prisoners and, as far as Kyle knew, was still in solitary – and had been for several years.

'You're kidding. Why him?'

'After his last appeal fell on deaf ears the powers-that-be decided to allocate a case worker to see if some of his needs and concerns could be addressed. I am that case worker.'

Kyle mulled it over. 'He's one of a kind, so I've heard. He was abused himself as a child, and as far as I recall he's always maintained that his violence is directed not at his victims, but at mental images of his dysfunctional parents.'

'Yes, that's what he told me, among other things. He's actually a sensitive guy, into art, music, philosophy. But for the last few years he hasn't been allowed books, music, anything.'

'That's not something I'd lose sleep over.'

'Well, that's where I've been able to help. I've been able to get alongside him, assess his mental state, try to make his life if not better, then at least bearable.'

'You're the best Good Samaritan I know.'

'Don't you think he deserves to be treated like a human being? He's been locked up in a bulletproof cage twenty-three hours a day. Nothing to read, nothing to listen to, except his own thoughts. It would drive anyone crazy.'

Kyle nodded. 'If you want my opinion, I think he's made

his bed. He's lucky the death sentence was abolished.'

'But it has been. And he's alive. That's the point. Do you know, they even refused his request to end his life voluntarily?'

'Well, that's hardly a surprise. A bill to sanction voluntary suicide in Her Majesty's prisons isn't going to cut much ice in Parliament, is it? Even if it would solve the overcrowding problem.'

She looked at him and a deep frown appeared on her smooth forehead. 'He's not thinking like that anymore. He's in a normal cell, he has some privileges. He's very grateful.'

'You're quite something. He doesn't know how lucky he is. But why are you telling me all this?'

'I … I just wanted to know what you thought. As a serving police officer—'

'*Ex*-serving police officer. And what do you mean? What do I think about what, exactly?'

She clicked her tongue, frustrated. 'This is all new territory to me. I've never dealt with someone like this before, Cam. I just wanted to sound you out. You're a sensitive guy. Well, that is …' she looked puzzled, 'you *were*. You seem a bit … different.'

'I do?'

'Yes. You're … I don't know. More … direct.'

'Yep. They told me to expect a few changes in the personality department. I'm still working through it.'

'Of course. Anyway, I thought you might have some advice, you know, as to how to read him.'

'Read him? Well, my advice would be … don't let him get under your skin. He'll be playing you for all the sympathy he can get.'

'Don't *trust* him, you mean?'

'Just watch your back. And whatever you do, Bec—'

She searched his face. 'What?'

'Make sure the warders are close by. At all times. Do *not* let them out of your sight.'

'Yeah, I'm careful. But he wouldn't lay a hand on me. We have a good rapport going.'

'That's what he wants you to think.' He looked at her, already more worried than he was willing to admit. '*Never*, and I mean *never*, turn your back on him.'

'You don't think someone like that can change, do you?'

Kyle shook his head. 'No,' he said. 'Frankly, I don't.'

Chapter Three

Kyle walked the short distance back to his apartment lost in thought. Rebecca's unexpected visit had unsettled him. Even though he'd been preoccupied with his health, she'd never been far from his mind, and although he felt pleased that she'd come to him for advice, he was confused by her easy manner with him. Their relationship had ended badly; emotions had run high, he'd said some things he now regretted, as had she. Now she seemed to have swept all that under the carpet. Was that normal?

He found his keys and let himself in. Why had she confided in him? Why had she felt it necessary to sound him out?

It wasn't long – less than 24 hours, in fact – before he had an answer.

He was woken early the following morning by an insistent knocking. He'd been deep in a surreal dream where he was being operated on by a team of policemen using knitting needles as scalpels, each taking a turn to have a poke around in his brain. His head was throbbing when consciousness returned and it took him a full half-minute to come to and a further minute to persuade his eyes to open.

The banging that had woken him was becoming more persistent. The HSC would have to wait – whoever was at the door clearly wasn't prepared to do the same.

'All *right*. Hold on. I'm coming.'

He unbolted the front door, swung it open, stepped back a pace. 'What on *Earth*?'

'Morning, DC Kyle. I'm sure you don't need to see our warrant cards.'

'It's six in the morning.' Kyle ignored DI Patterson's assumption. 'What the hell do you want?'

'A word. May we?'

Kyle didn't recognise Patterson's accompanying officer. His replacement, perhaps? She was around his age, attractive. Her neutral expression was giving nothing away, but she had dark rings under her eyes. Not an early riser, then, or perhaps Patterson was just overworking her – it was something he was known for. 'Nice to meet you,' he told her. 'You'd better come in.'

Kyle led them into the lounge, dropped into an armchair, waved them to the sofa. 'This had better be good. I've been told I need rest.'

'Indeed. So, how are you?' Patterson went for a sympathetic smile, but sympathy had never been one of his strong points.

'Alive.'

Patterson nodded. 'Bloody lucky, you were. I should count my blessings if I were you.'

'Closest friend dead. That's a blessing?'

'It's a blessing you're still with us,' the female officer said.

'Sorry – this is DC Bates.' Patterson jerked his thumb at Kyle. 'And this is DC Kyle.'

'*Ex*-DC Kyle.'

Patterson ran a hand through his hair, a habitual gesture.

'I'll get straight to it,' he said. 'What was Rebecca Wilson doing here yesterday morning?'

'What's that got to do with anything?'

'You know the form,' Patterson growled. 'Answer the question.'

Unlike Patterson, DC Bates hadn't sat down. She was moving slowly around the apartment, taking it all in. Looking for evidence. Kyle had done it himself. He knew the form. 'She wanted to see how I was.' Kyle shrugged. 'We were an item. Once.'

'I know. That's why I think she might have confided in you.'

'About what?'

Patterson leaned forward. 'About Kenneth Munday.'

Kyle's heart missed a beat. 'What's happened?'

'Ah, so she did mention him?'

'Tell me what's happened.' Kyle squinted as a knot of pain throbbed in his temple.

Bates joined Patterson on the sofa. 'The truth is, Mr Kyle, we don't know. That's why we'd like to find out what she said to you yesterday.'

'OK, so she talked about Munday. She wondered whether I thought a man could change in prison, turn over a new leaf.'

'Are you all right?' Bates frowned. 'You look pale. Shall I get you some water?'

'I'm fine. I just have a permanent headache. Some days are worse than others. Look, all I told her is that guys like Munday don't change – and to be careful. In my opinion, any apparent reform is likely to be a sham. Now would you kindly tell me what all this is about?'

Patterson folded his arms. 'All right. Yesterday evening at around six pm, Kenneth Munday absconded from HMP Fairview, accompanied by Rebecca Wilson. All attempts to locate them – so far – have come to naught.'

Chapter Four

Kyle gripped the arm of his chair. 'How? He's a high-security prisoner.' His head swam with lurid scenarios, ghastly possibilities.

'We're still trying to establish exactly what happened, DC Kyle,' Bates said.

'Will you *stop* calling me that?' Kyle was on his feet now, pacing the room.

'That's why we've come knocking,' Patterson added with a close-lipped smile. 'To see if you can enlighten us. Perhaps Ms Wilson mentioned something. You know the sort of thing. Have a think.'

'I'll tell you what I'm thinking. I'm wondering why you're wasting time here when a psychotic multiple murderer has absconded with a good friend of mine.' Kyle stopped pacing, rubbed his eyes. A kaleidoscope of colours flashed against his retinas. When he blinked, coloured dots peppered his vision then slowly dispersed as he refocused on the two detectives.

'Take it easy,' Patterson said. 'Have a seat. Last thing you should be doing is getting yourself worked up.'

'Thanks for the reminder.' Kyle sank back into the chair, exhaled. 'Look, there's nothing else. That's all she told me. She's assigned to him as a case worker.' A thought occurred to him. 'You used the word 'accompanied'. So, she left the prison with him voluntarily? She wasn't abducted at knifepoint? Or–'

'Like I said,' Bates interrupted, 'we're still trying to establish the facts.'

'But you must know *something*, surely? Witnesses? I mean–'

Patterson and Bates exchanged glances. Patterson said, 'She was authorised to take Munday to the prison library. They were escorted. There was some kind of … mix up, a distraction. Next thing they know, Munday and Wilson are outside. We think they got away in Wilson's Morris; every squad car we have is out there looking for it. But like I said – so far, nothing.' Patterson's eyes scanned the room. 'Mind if I have a look around?'

'Be my guest.'

Patterson went into the hall.

'Don't suppose there's any chance of a brew?' Bates pursed her lips and looked hopeful.

'Sure.' Kyle went through to the kitchen and Bates followed.

She watched him opening cupboards, finding mugs. 'The guv was right. You are a big bloke.'

'Six two.'

'Rugby player?'

'Yes.' Kyle clicked the kettle button. 'But not at present.'

'I'm sorry. About what happened.'

'Yeah?' Kyle spooned tea into the teapot. One for the pot, one for himself and Bates. Patterson could make his own.

'Your friend. That's … a tough call.'

'Yep.'

'I'm sure it wasn't your fault.'

Kyle opened the fridge door, grabbed a carton of milk. 'Are you? How's that?'

Bates looked taken aback. 'Well, I just am. I mean, it could happen to anyone.'

'What did Patterson tell you?' He handed her a mug. Its design featured a graphic of a rising sun and the strap line *Good Morning Sunshine – enjoy your day!* emblazoned in yellow.

'Honestly? Well...'

'It's OK. I'm thick-skinned.'

'That's not what he said. He said you were ... a gentle giant. Too gentle for a copper, anyway.'

'Inhibited? Too careful? Lacking in confidence?'

Bates played with the mug, avoided eye contact. 'Close, but...'

'But what?'

'But I'm not getting that now.' She looked at him appraisingly. 'I wouldn't have said confidence was an issue.'

'Wouldn't you? So you know me pretty well, then.' Kyle refilled the teapot, gave it a stir.

'Look, I don't mean to be presumptuous – I'm just saying what I see. Anyway, good for you,' Bates said. 'It takes more guts to tackle the bad stuff if you have confidence issues.'

Kyle felt unexpectedly touched. No one had ever said anything like that to him before. He looked at Bates dumbly.

He was saved from further conversation by Patterson. 'Two sugars, please,' the DI said as he came into the kitchen. 'Have to be quick, though – I want a catch-up with Traffic. They must have some news on Wilson's car by now or I'll want to know why.'

Chapter Five

The Italian glanced up as the messenger came in. He was just a boy, seventeen, maybe eighteen. Parents both in prison, no siblings, a history of petty crime that had threatened to escalate into something more sordid to make ends meet. Munday had taken him under his wing, and he had proved a faithful gopher; the Italian had worried briefly about his loyalties after Munday had been sentenced, but the boy seemed happy to work for a new master, and the Italian was invariably generous to happy, reliable, faithful workers.

'Hello Tony. What can I do for you?'

The boy came up to the desk but remained standing. Good manners. The Italian approved.

Tony cleared his throat. 'I just heard. Thought you should know. He's out. Ken's got 'imself free.'

'I see. Well, that *is* good news.'

The boy looked pleased. And why shouldn't he? Munday had been something of a saviour to him. Perversely, the Italian found a tune from the atheist Verdi's *Quattro Pezzi Sacri* on his lips. He hummed a few stanzas while the boy shuffled his feet, looked at the floor.

'And your source?'

'The usual. It's good.'

The Italian nodded. 'I'm sure.' Sources were only reliable when they had proved themselves to be so – and, once

43

proven, the Italian was content to reuse them again and again.

So, Munday was out, and he would be looking to consolidate his assets. But here was the problem: Munday had been gaoled before he could communicate the location of his various assets, and since he had been a guest of Her Majesty he had declined to pass on that knowledge. This was an annoyance, a stone in each of the Italian's expensive shoes. It was a situation that needed resolving. Perhaps now was the time to invest some thought into how the situation might be rectified. A day or two, perhaps, to allow the dust of Munday's illegal egress to settle. A day or two for him to make plans to secure his assets.

And, on the Italian's part, a watchful eye, until an appropriate moment presented itself.

'Is there anything else?' The boy Tony was looking at the desk, hoovering up any information he could interpret from the various inverted letters and notepapers. The Italian let it pass. Tony was learning, honing his skills. That was good; skills could be mobilised when necessary. As long as he remained loyal, the Italian was happy to indulge and encourage. Loyalty was paramount.

The Italian found his wallet, opened it and withdrew a five pound note, passed it across the desk.

'With my thanks.'

The boy did a good job trying to disguise his surprise, but his delight was obvious. He nodded and left the room on light feet.

The Italian smiled.

Loyalty in action.

Kyle was fighting a feeling of dread. If they found Rebecca's car in a ditch somewhere, or—

Bates picked up on his anxiety. 'I expect Munday'll let her go, once he's put a few miles between himself and Fairview.' Bates sipped her tea. She caught Kyle's expression and added, 'I'm sure she'll be fine.'

'Time to go, DC Bates.' Patterson set his mug down with a bang, nodded in Kyle's direction. 'Much obliged.'

'I'm coming with you.'

'I think not.' Patterson jabbed a finger. '*You* are staying put, DC Kyle.'

'*Ex*-D—'

'Whatever.' Patterson waved the correction away. 'In the meantime, if you remember anything helpful, you know where to find me.'

'If you think I'm going to sit around while—'

'Best leave it with us.' Bates shot him a warning smile, but there was more behind it than just 'back off'. It implied a degree of collusion. Kyle fell silent.

He showed the two detectives to the front door where Bates threw him a final over-the-shoulder glance. She didn't exactly wink, but he got the message. He had an ally.

Patterson fired a parting shot. 'You won't hear anything on the news yet, Kyle. If I catch the slightest whiff the story's got out, I'll know whose balls to serve up to the Chief Constable. Got that?'

'Just do your job, Patterson.'

'I intend to.' Patterson rested his hand lightly on DC Bates' arm. 'And DC Bates here is a quick learner – we make a good team.' Kyle noted Bates' reaction in the quick intake of breath, the way she pulled sharply away from the DI's touch.

Kyle shut the door, backtracked to the kitchen and retrieved his mug of tea. There was an annotated scrap of notebook paper next to the coffee jar on the work surface. A phone number. Kyle was impressed; Bates' score on his empathy scale was firmly at the top.

But empathy wasn't going to find Rebecca. She was a killer's hostage, and he didn't intend to cool his heels waiting around for news.

Kyle went through to the lounge and sat down. *OK, let's think this through.*

DC Bates was probably right; Munday would probably let Rebecca go once he was clear of London. But if that had happened she would have been in touch by now, either with the police or, quite possibly given their recent conversation, with him directly. Which meant that Munday was still holding her somewhere. Kyle examined the tea leaves at the bottom of his mug. Even with a fine strainer, somehow there were always a few that escaped. Maybe he should treat himself to a new one.

But the tea leaves remained silent and Kyle's thoughts careered forward like a runaway roller-coaster. What if Munday had taken another course of action altogether? What if he had *never* planned to release her?

Best not dwell on that. Best consider how he had escaped in the first place. How had Munday planned it? The clue had to be in Rebecca's questions; Munday had gained her trust, judged his moment, but the prison staff must have been daydreaming big time to drop the ball so spectacularly. Kyle didn't envy them, nor the prison governor. Heads would undoubtedly roll, whatever the outcome.

Munday had had plenty of time to figure out rotas, staff allocations, busy and quiet times of day, the best routes ... in short, everything he needed to plan his exit. Accomplices must have been involved too, Kyle reasoned. Anything was possible inside; he'd seen it before. The corruption, the bribes, the threats.

His head was throbbing. Tea didn't help in that respect, but it stimulated his thinking. And thinking was what Kyle was good at, whatever else Patterson might believe. He went back to the kitchen, poured another cup.

His phone rang.

He went into the hall and picked up the receiver. 'Yes?'

'Hi. This is Sven Jörgensen. I'm sorry to trouble you but I need to speak with you urgently. The police have been here. Is it convenient to call round?'

Kyle kept his voice nice and reasonable. 'Sure.'

'OK. Thanks. Bye.'

Concise and to the point. Kyle replaced the receiver.

So Patterson had already covered the boyfriend angle. First port of call, probably. But Kyle saw no reason not to talk to Jörgensen. They'd only met once, awkwardly, in town, a few months after he and Rebecca had split; he'd done his best to be civil to the pair of them, but the encounter had left him in a state of flux and regret. Jörgensen had clocked it, made some excuse about a late appointment and they'd hurried off. There'd been no backward glance from Rebecca. He'd finished his shopping trip with a heavy heart. Seeing your ex with a new partner; that made it real.

The tea tasted faintly of almonds. His tastebuds had significantly altered since the bullet; Winder hadn't mentioned that. Sweet things sometimes tasted sour and vice-versa. He'd never liked oranges before; now he ate at least two a day.

The doorbell rang. He looked at the kitchen clock; seven-thirty. Postman, probably.

He opened the front door to Sven Jörgensen.

'Cameron,' Jörgensen offered a forced smile. 'I'm sorry to trouble you.' He registered Kyle's surprise. 'I called from the phone box outside. I wanted to check you were OK with this before I visited.'

'Well, you're here now.' Kyle let him in without offering a handshake. He could see that Jörgensen was in a state of nervous excitement. 'I'm assuming you know what's happened?'

'I know more than that,' Jörgensen said. 'I know where she is.'

Chapter Six

'Someone called me at five this morning. A man. He said, if I want her back I have to bring £2,000 in cash, single bag. Alone. No police. No clever moves. Weald Hall Estate, on the Essex border. By the west side of the lake, he said, there's a staircase. He'll meet me there. I have the money, that's not a problem. But I want you to come with me.'

'Did you tell Patterson?'

'No. I don't want to risk getting them involved. You and me, we can go and get her. Then it's all done.'

Kyle looked Jörgensen up and down. He was a classic-looking Swede. Blond hair in need of a trim, gold-rimmed spectacles. A slim-fit jacket that looked just a shade small for him, a bag slung over one shoulder as per the European standard, a shirt that didn't look like any shirt you could pick up in a Hepworth's menswear section.

'It won't be all done,' Kyle told him. 'This sort of thing never is. And the caller is dodgy on at least two counts.'

'What do you mean?'

Kyle sighed. 'Two grand? For a guy like Munday that's chickenfeed. Why bother? Rumour has it he's got caches of loot dotted around the country like party favours.' Kyle shook his head. 'He doesn't need money.'

'Then what?'

'If not the money, then it's you.'

'What? Why?'

'You're a lawyer, right? Tell me, was Munday ever a client of yours?'

Jörgensen's silence was affirmation enough.

'So, I'm guessing your defence case crumbled and he wasn't too happy with you. Neither would I be if I had to spend the next thirty-odd years inside.'

Jörgensen had taken off his glasses, was polishing them with a red cloth. 'You're right. He was a client. And no, it didn't go well.'

'Munday will be wanting a little chat with you.'

'You think he wants to *kill* me?' Jörgensen nodded slowly. 'But...' The Swede looked around Kyle's lounge as if searching for a way out of his predicament. 'If I don't go, he might hurt Rebecca. And If I *do* go, then–'

'Yep. He has you over the proverbial barrel.' Kyle picked a chair and sank heavily into it. 'But you'd already figured that. That's why you came to see me.'

Jörgensen perched on the edge of the sofa, retied a lace. 'You're right. But what else could I do? He straightened his back. 'You care about Rebecca, I know that.'

'You're the last person I'd want to discuss that with.'

'Sure, sure, I get it. Sorry to mention it.'

Kyle's head was still thumping like a trip hammer. 'Maybe calling Patterson *is* your best option.'

'You won't come with me?' Jörgensen looked distraught.

'Perhaps you're not aware of my situation,' Kyle said. 'Let me explain...'

When he'd finished, Jörgensen sat quietly for a moment. 'A bullet? My God...' he trailed off until another thought occurred to him. 'But, we can negotiate, yes? We don't have to resort to violence.'

Kyle wanted to laugh. 'Violence is Munday's first call. He doesn't understand anything else.'

Jörgensen snorted. 'No, you're right. A difficult man, as I well remember.' He brightened. 'I could offer three thousand? I can get a loan...'

'Forget it. The money's irrelevant.'

Jörgensen made an exasperated gesture. 'If I call Patterson, you know what will happen. They'll send in armed police, make a big mess, and Rebecca ... man, I just can't take that risk.'

Kyle considered. Jörgensen was probably right; he'd been involved in similar operations and they were hazardous in the extreme – to both perpetrator and victim.

But Rebecca ... he couldn't leave it to Patterson. And he couldn't let Jörgensen screw things up, either.

Jörgensen was watching him carefully. 'Hey, just forget it, all right? I'll figure this out on my own.' The Swede stood up.

'No, you won't. You're a lawyer. Lawyers belong in courtrooms and offices.'

Jörgensen bristled. 'You'd better be care—'

Kyle cut him off. 'Weald Hall rings a bell.'

Jörgensen took out an envelope, waved it in Kyle's face. 'This was left in my letterbox this morning an hour after the phone call.'

The front of the envelope bore a single word written in biro: 'Jörgensen'.

'Open it.'

Jörgensen strode to Kyle's desk, picked up a letter opener, slit the envelope and withdrew a single sheet of folded paper.

It was an article cut out from a magazine or newspaper. Jörgensen scanned it, made an exasperated noise and handed it to Kyle.

Kyle skimmed the text:

Weald Hall *was originally a stately home built by the Victorian fraudster and fantasist, AG Barry ... who constructed two man-made lakes in the grounds. Beneath the first he built an underground ballroom from where guests could view the lake and its fish while enjoying dancing and socialising. The room is entered via a narrow tunnel ... still intact today although in poor condition ... estate is due to be redeveloped by the National Trust ... out of bounds to the public in the meantime ... the Trust hope in the near future to ....*

At the foot of the article someone had added: *Be there, Jörgensen. Soon.*

'OK. Now we know.' Kyle considered the route. 'A couple of hours should do it.'

'I guess.' Jörgensen glared, still smarting from Kyle's blunt dismissal. 'Are you going to help or not?'

'Think of me as your invisible partner. We don't have to be nice to each other.'

'But what are we going to *do*?'

'I have no idea,' Kyle said truthfully. 'You drive, I'll think.'

As they left the apartment, Kyle wondered about his own state of mind. He was aware that a mental shift had taken place, almost without his being aware of it. As Winder had warned, it appeared that his usual caution had been substituted for an unfamiliar spontaneity, almost as though his inhibitions had been rerouted to some redundant cranial siding. However, as long as the change continued to have a positive effect, Kyle was content to go with it – the trick, he suspected, was not to dwell on it.

'It's the gold Jaguar, by Fine Fare.' Jörgensen jangled his keys.

'Nice,' Kyle said. 'But then you lawyers can afford the best, right?'

Jörgensen got into the driver's seat without a word. Kyle folded himself into the passenger's side and fastened his seat belt; these cars could move. The Swede eased the XJ6 into the traffic and Kyle felt the acceleration push him into the seat.

With a stab of guilt, he wondered how DC Bates was getting on. He was about to go off-piste, big time, but he felt he owed it to her to keep her abreast of developments. Not Patterson. Stuff Patterson.

On reflection, maybe it would be wise to see how things panned out at Weald Hall before getting back in touch. He had her number if he needed it.

In the meantime, off-piste was off-piste.

Chapter Seven

The Italian tapped his fountain pen lightly on the desktop. Munday had made an error. The English had an expression: if you want something doing properly, do it yourself. It was a good maxim. The Italian approved. The English were sadly lacking in many areas, but their proverbs usually hit the mark.

Hit the mark...

There was another. The Italian always aimed to *hit the mark*. But now was not the time to intervene. It would be prudent to wait, to allow events to unfold in the way he knew they inevitably would.

He stood up, a languid, easy movement, rolled his shoulders. Too much desk work made him sluggish, and that was undesirable. Of course it was important to attend to the minutiae, the necessary paperwork, but the Italian preferred to be active.

He moved to the bay window, looked out onto the street. A bus rumbled by, wipers fighting a losing battle with the steady rain. Pedestrians hurried along the pavements, heads bent beneath an assortment of umbrellas, newspapers or, in the case of the elderly ladies, oddly flapping and ineffectual rain hats, folded strips of polythene held on by a string. What an eccentric race the English were, helpless slaves to their damp and inhospitable climate.

The Italian stretched, let out his breath in a long sigh. He missed the sun, the lifestyle, the music of his native country, but he had come to England for a reason; it was the land of opportunity. A country where he found himself able to fruitfully ply his trade week after week, month after month. There was no limit. Information was readily available. Businessmen here were careless, easily compromised. It was like ... what was the English expression? *Falling off a log*. The Italian smiled. That was perfect. That was exactly how it was.

Kenneth Munday had been one of his first contacts. For a while the Italian had been content to remain on the sidelines, listening, learning, gaining an understanding of the culture. Munday had been a good teacher. They were very different, but their skills were complementary. It had been a good partnership until Munday had grown careless. The Italian had sensed the danger, stepped back before the net had closed.

And Munday had left a space, a gap that needed filling. The Italian was his obvious successor; no one questioned it. He was aware of the fear in Munday's men's eyes as he spoke to them, told them what he expected, but fear was a persuasive incentive. He didn't care if they disliked him. This was business, after all, not a social club. They belonged to him now. And so, accordingly, he had had them branded. A proof of loyalty. None had refused.

The Italian turned away from the grey view, returned to his exquisite Maggiolini bureau, and sat down. He picked up the stiletto, tested its point with his forefinger, inspected the result. A minute drop of blood had appeared on his fingertip. He removed it with his tongue.

Enough introspection. There was work to be done. The Italian hummed a musical phrase from Puccini's *Nessun Dorma*. What was the translation?

Ah, yes. *None shall sleep.*

It was an appropriate thought to carry forward into the day.

Chapter Eight

'So, what happened?'

Kyle clicked his tongue in irritation. 'Context?'

'Your bullet. What else?'

Kyle closed his eyes. 'Why do you want to know?'

'I'm curious. It was a bad situation, obviously.' Jörgensen overtook a dawdling lorry. Unusually, traffic on the North Circular Road was moving at a relatively brisk pace. They should arrive at Weald Hall at around four pm, which would give them a few hours of daylight to have a snoop around. Or maybe they should wait until dusk.

Kyle kept his eyes shut, said, 'I'm not sure I want to talk about it.'

'Come on, man. Rebecca says talking stuff through is the best therapy.' He shot Kyle a sideways glance.

'With you? I think not.'

'It was a gang, right? Extortionists? That's what the papers said. But you didn't expect them to use a gun...' Jörgensen took a quick intake of breath. 'I guess it took you by surprise, huh?'

'You could say that.'

'You lost a friend. Sorry about that.'

'Thanks.'

'So, was it your call?'

'Let's just focus on the job in hand.'

Jörgensen shrugged. 'Sure. But you shouldn't get involved physically, that much is clear.' He pulled a face. 'What is less clear is what I'm going to find when I get there. Do I just hand over the money?'

'He'll let us know.'

'So I give him the money, and then he kills me?'

'That's where I come in. If you give me time to think, maybe I'll figure something out.'

'And what if they do something to Rebecca?'

'Same answer.'

'Tell me one thing.'

'What?'

'The gang got away? The guy with the shooter?'

Kyle sighed. The slang sounded odd coming from the mouth of a Swede. 'They'll be caught. Eventually.'

'Not much of a consolation, huh?'

'No.'

'But, at least—'

'Just drop it, OK?'

'OK, sure. No problem.' Jörgensen hit the accelerator as they exited a restricted speed zone and the Jag leapt forward. They drove in silence for ten minutes.

'She'll be all right. She's tough,' Jörgensen said.

Kyle already knew that. But tough might fall short when dealing with people like Munday. Especially now, when the lifer would be unpredictable, untrustworthy, desperate. Kyle had been toying with the idea of calling it in. One call to Bates and that would be that. But Patterson? He didn't trust him; The DI would focus on Munday and any collateral damage would be a sub-paragraph in his report. *Regrettable,*

but inevitable, given the severity of the situation...
And so on.
So, no call.
Jörgensen repeated his statement. 'I said, she's tough. I'm not worried.'
'I heard you.'
'You have a plan yet?'
'Working on it.'
Jörgensen pressed on. 'You were a cop. You must have done this before. I mean, blackmail, kidnap, all that stuff. You must have an idea how to approach a situation like this.'
'Must I?'
Jörgensen shook his head. 'You don't give much away, do you?'
'I try not to.'
'Well, it's forty minutes before we get there. You'd better keep thinking.'
'Rebecca talk to you about Munday?'
'Sure.' Jörgensen nodded. 'Actually, I'd already told her about him. I knew he was in Fairview. She was interested, so I told her about the case. Not one of my successes, but memorable, that's for sure.'
'Did he ever try it on with you? You know, offer a bribe, anything else to strengthen his case?'
'Not really.'
'OK.'
'Why?'
'I'm just trying to get a picture of the man, figure out how he thinks.'
It actually wasn't too hard to figure. Abused and let down by social care, Munday, like so many, had fallen through the

cracks and gone full out for his only remaining option: crime. And then, after the inevitable imprisonment, a vigilante double-whammy when he'd lured two fellow-prisoners into his cell and coolly despatched them, one at a time, for their misdeeds. Twisted justice, acting out his revenge against the parents he'd never be able to execute in reality. The two victims had both committed crimes of abuse, and that had been enough for Munday. Years in solitary had followed, until one day a case worker with a soft heart and a determined streak had walked into his cell and said, "You know what, Mr Munday? You've suffered alone long enough. I'm here to help. First, rehabilitation within the prison. After that … it's up to you."

Rebecca. Always ready to see the best in people, even scumbags like Munday, always ready to fight their corner. Too trusting by far.

'If you don't have a plan, I'm going to do what I have to do.' Jörgensen indicated, pulled off at the junction. They cruised to a roundabout, waited at the lights.

'And what might that be?' Kyle asked.

Jörgensen patted his coat pocket. 'First chance I get, I'm going to blow the bastard's head off.'

Chapter Nine

'Interesting character, Kyle,' Bates said as they pulled up behind the squad car. 'How long did he work for you?' Patterson yanked the handbrake. 'Eighteen months or so. He's a bright fella, just overcautious.'

'He didn't come over like that just now.'

Patterson paused, his hand on the door release. 'Trauma does odd things to the mind. If you want my honest opinion, he's better off out of it. Wrong personality for a copper.'

Bates inclined her head. 'If you say so.'

Patterson was already out of the vehicle, striding towards the traffic officer who, judging from his expression, was keen to hand over responsibility and get on his way. Bates did a slow three-sixty around Wilson's car while Patterson got the lowdown from Traffic. She pulled on plastic gloves, opened the passenger door, stuck her head inside. It was clean – cleaner than clean. Spotless; no personal items in sight. Bates opened the glove box. A map of London, an A4 sheet with the recovery company's telephone number, an AA handbook. She closed the door and joined Patterson.

'No sign of a struggle. Clean as a whistle,' she told him.

'Appreciate you calling this in.' Patterson thanked the Traffic officer and they watched as he and his colleague drove away.

'Time for some neighbourly calls,' Bates suggested.

'Someone might have seen them.'

'We have to assume a change of cars,' Patterson said, half to himself. 'Munday could well have had one laid on.'

'It never ceases to amaze me what they can do from inside,' Bates said. 'I mean, how do they organise something like this?'

'Visiting times, letters, phone calls. Coded instructions.'

'Unless Wilson set it up for him, of course.'

Patterson raised an eyebrow.

Bates hooked a strand of hair over her ear. A fresh gust of wind immediately undid the operation and she gave in, let it blow freely. 'What if he threatened her?'

'She was either coerced or complicit. I'd say the former, in which case, yes, he may well have done.'

'Where would you go? I mean, if you were an escapee.'

Bates moved back a step. Patterson was doing his usual thing, invading her personal space.

Patterson put his hands in his raincoat pockets. 'I'd lie low for a few weeks, then try to leave the country.'

Bates pursed her lips, nodded. 'I'm worried we haven't heard from Wilson. Why is he hanging on to her?'

'Bargaining power if we catch up with him, that's the most likely reason.'

'The boyfriend. What did you make of him?'

Patterson sniffed. 'Not a lot. Seemed a bit wet. Limp-wristed, lawyer type.'

'Not biased, then.' Bates smiled. 'Against the legal profession ... or Nordics in general?'

'Not at all, DC Bates.' Patterson maintained his innocent expression. He tapped her on the shoulder. 'Let's get to it. You start on the neighbours, I'll get the Morris towed away.'

Forensics can take it to bits. You never know, something might drop out.'

'Got it.'

Relieved to put distance between them, Bates turned and surveyed the row of semi-detacheds. Patterson was way too touchy-feely for her liking. It had started innocuously enough, just the occasional hand on her arm, a lingering eye contact, but over the last few weeks... Bates took a deep breath. Her parents had warned her that the male-dominated Met was not the place for a young girl, but it was what she wanted – had always wanted, ever since she was little. There had been no doubt in her mind that one day she would realise her dream and become a policewoman. And her parents had been *so* proud of her when she'd told them that she was being considered for a detective role. Up to now she'd been able to handle the comments, the innuendos, but Patterson ... he was something else.

Come on, DC Bates. Job in hand...

With a conscious effort she returned her attention to the case. Munday was probably hundreds of miles away by now. They were, what, two miles from Fairview? So they'd have parked up around six twenty, allowing for rush hour traffic. How observant were residents at home time? Not very, in Bates' experience. Returning commuters would have their minds set on pre-dinner drinks, unwinding, catching the kids before bedtime.

Still, it was worth a shot. She approached the nearest house and knocked on the door.

A well-dressed, middle-aged woman opened it.

'Oh.' The woman took a step back. 'Not the window-cleaners. Can I help?'

Bates gave a brief explanation.

'The Morris?' She peered into the street where Patterson was leaning on Wilson's car, watching the exchange. 'Yes, I did notice it. It's not a resident's car, and I'm good at spotting that kind of thing. We like to keep a watchful eye open. You can't be too careful these days, what with—'

Bates interrupted the flow with a raised finger. 'I wonder, did you see who was driving? The passenger, maybe?'

'A big fellow, and a woman. I'm not sure who was driving. When I saw them they were standing exactly where that man is now.' She pointed to Patterson. '*She* looked a little flustered when the other chap arrived.'

'Other chap?'

'Yes. Another man pulled up, and she got in with him.'

'And the man she was with? The first man, I mean?'

The woman knitted her brow. She was heavily made-up, a caked layer of foundation and too much lipstick. Papering over the cracks, Bates' father would have called it.

'I *think* … yes, yes, he just walked off.'

'Really?' That was a turn up, Munday taking off on foot.

'Do you happen to remember the make and colour of the second car, the one that pulled up?'

'I'm not the best at car models,' the woman confessed. 'But it was blue, I think, a saloon – not an estate.'

'And did the woman get in the car willingly, do you think? Or—'

The woman compressed her lips. 'He held her arm, but … no, she didn't put up a fight or anything like that…'

Bates fished for a card. 'If you remember anything else, would you mind giving me a call?'

'Of course, dear. Such good work, our police do.'

Bates gave her a smile. 'We try.'

'I hope you catch them, whatever they've done.' The woman frowned. 'We live in a troubled society these days, don't we? All these long-haired louts. They need to bring back National Service, that's what my John always says.'

Bates reprised her tolerant smile. 'Thanks for your help, madam.'

She carried on with the next few houses, but no one else had seen anything untoward either. She backtracked along the street and rejoined Patterson who was standing, hands in pockets, while a police recovery vehicle secured Wilson's car in preparation for its journey to Forensics.

Bates raised her voice above the beat of the recovery vehicle's engine, told Patterson what she'd learned.

He nodded, yelled back. 'OK, so we're thinking Wilson switched cars, and Munday strolled away on Shank's pony? Why would he do that? Unless there was another vehicle waiting around the corner?'

'Rush hour.' Bates shrugged. 'Easy to get lost in the underground crowds. Maybe.'

Patterson blew his cheeks out. 'This gets worse every minute. OK, next stop for you is to ask around at the nearest Tube.'

'And the guy Wilson took off with?'

Patterson made a face. 'I'm not gifted with second-sight, DC Bates. One step at a time. Meet me back at base in, say, a couple of hours. Call me if you find anything.'

Patterson got into his car and pulled out at a speed that said a lot for his current frame of mind. Bates took a deep breath. At least she had some solitary respite. She took out her London A to Z and headed off to find the local Tube station.

Chapter Ten

'I strongly suggest you leave that in the car,' Kyle said. 'This isn't the Wild West, and I'll bet you've never fired anything in anger other than a junior solicitor.'

'So, what do I do? Walk in and he pops me? End of story?'

They were parked on a service road next to the abandoned Weald Hall estate. To their immediate right, a crumbling wall and overgrown iron gate offered a less than inviting portal into the unknown.

'Bring the money,' Kyle advised. 'We can wave it at them. It might buy us a few seconds when we need it. We go in together.'

'That's it? That's your plan?'

'I'll improvise as we go.' Kyle opened the door, clambered out, stretched his legs. In spite of his concerns regarding Bec's welfare, it felt good to be doing something.

Jörgensen looked daggers at him across the Jag's roof. 'If anything happens to Rebecca, I'll know who to blame.'

'If anything happens, you'll probably be dead, so I wouldn't worry about it.'

Without waiting for a reply Kyle headed for the gates. A lop-sided warning sign in faded capitals was roughly fastened to the metalwork by a rusty chain which also held the gates closed. There was no lock; Kyle unravelled the chain, heaved the gate open a few inches, just enough to squeeze through.

Ahead lay an overgrown path. Kyle took it, barrelling through bushes and brushing foliage aside as he went. He could hear Jörgensen's tentative tread a few yards behind, keeping his distance, playing it safe. Kyle knew there was no *safe* in situations like this, but neither was there any mileage in being overly cautious. Those days, he realised with a mixture of surprise and ambivalence, were gone.

The path widened into a large open area delimited by birch and aspen and dominated by an oval ornamental lake. The green-tinted water lay flat under the grey April sky and at the far end a magnificent willow tree dipped its branches into the depths. Half-way along, on the west side of the water, a rusted, metallic arch drew Kyle's eye.

By the west side of the lake there's a staircase. Go down it.

'What if they just shoot us while we're in the open?'

'Any more what ifs and I'll shoot you myself,' Kyle said. 'They invited you, remember?'

The neglected lawn was soft and mulchy under his feet as Kyle strode towards the archway. He could see why Munday had chosen the spot; the only inhabitants of this long-abandoned estate lived in trees and burrows. Screened by a row of poplars, the derelict stately home was just visible in the near distance. Kyle caught a glimpse of dark, brooding windows, long since deglazed, the house presiding over the lake like a gloomy spirit from a bygone age.

Jörgensen caught him by the shoulder as Kyle was about to descend. 'Are you crazy? Shouldn't we at least wait until dark?'

'You watch too many movies,' Kyle said, shrugging him off. 'I need to be sure of the environment. Trust me, it's a lot easier in daylight.'

'OK. You're in charge.'

Jörgensen didn't sound convinced, but Kyle wasn't going to lose any sleep over it.

They entered the art deco style walkway, Kyle leading, Jörgensen trailing behind. Maybe he thought it would give him an edge if they had to make a run for it. It wouldn't, not if firearms were involved. Kyle tried not to think about the last time he'd stepped in to a similarly volatile situation; he'd had Colin with him then – but now he was on his own. However, he still felt curiously indifferent to his own safety. It was Rebecca's life he wanted to preserve, even if it meant entrusting her to Jörgensen when this was over.

A rusting stairwell loomed in front of him. Kyle stopped and motioned for Jörgensen to do the same. He listened hard. The only sound was a light patter of rain on the roof; there was nothing to suggest anybody else was nearby.

Kyle began the descent. It was an odd sensation, the direction of the staircase confirming AG Barry's eccentric architectural ambition to build a sub-aquatic ballroom. Kyle tried to imagine the estate owner's party guests chattering excitedly as they filed along the tunnel in their finery, the lake above pressing down upon them like a sky full of heavy rain.

Kyle reached the bottom. It smelled dank and cold and the light had faded to an otherworldly greenish hue. Ahead was a short passageway, presumably leading to the ballroom. Now was the time to be cautious. He crept forward, stopped, listened carefully.

'Go on,' Jörgensen prompted from behind. 'Why have you stopped?'

Kyle half-turned to reply, but before he could say anything something metallic jabbed into the small of his back.

'That's right, I brought the gun anyway,' Jörgensen hissed. 'Now do as I say, and keep walking.'

Chapter Eleven

The first thing that struck Kyle as they entered the ballroom was not the sheer scale of the room, nor his uneasy awareness of the water above, but rather a huge sense of relief as he caught sight of Rebecca sitting demurely on an upturned crate at the far end of the room. Sure, he was angry with himself for walking into the trap, but at least he now knew what he was dealing with, and it wasn't Munday.

The guy walking towards them was roughly the same build, the same age – give or take – but it wasn't Fairview's erstwhile resident. So, unless the lifer was intending to make a theatrically late appearance, Kyle's opponents numbered two, and that wasn't bad odds – even if both men were armed.

Jörgensen gave him a shove and he staggered forward. Rebecca had sprung to her feet and was half-walking, half-running towards him. Her captor waved an automatic in her direction. 'That's far enough, darlin'.'

Rebecca stopped in her tracks. '*Cam!* I'm so sorry–' She looked behind him and caught sight of Jörgensen and her expression changed to one of confusion. '*Sven?* I … I don't understand…'

'You don't have to,' Jörgensen told her. 'So, both of you, back off to the wall. *Now*, please.' Jörgensen aimed his pistol directly at Rebecca. Kyle gave Rebecca an affirmative nod,

71

and they did as instructed.

Rebecca spoke in a terse whisper. 'Cam, what *is* this? What's happening?'

'Still trying to figure it out,' Kyle muttered. 'For now, just do what he says and keep your eyes peeled.'

The two men met in the centre of the room.

'That'll be mine, I think.' Rebecca's abductor waved the automatic at the bag in Sven's left hand.

Kyle clocked the droplets of sweat glistening on the man's forehead. Nervous, very nervous...

'Yes.' Sven made as if to hand the bag over. 'This is all for you.' As the older man reached for it, Jörgensen's other hand came up and the pistol barked once. The report echoed through the ballroom and reverberated along the connecting tunnels. The man stood stock still for several seconds as though he couldn't quite take in what had happened. Then, arms outstretched, he collapsed, the automatic clattering to the floor and spinning away towards the wall.

The Swede turned to face Kyle. 'And now you.'

Kyle put himself in front of Rebecca. 'What's the deal, Jörgensen? You and Munday? Let me guess – you offered to help him out for a small fee? What's your split? I hope it's worth it for the short time you'll have to enjoy it.'

Sven sidled up to them, the pistol secure in his grip. 'I'm not going to get caught, Kyle. I do things properly. I use my brain.' He tapped his forehead.

Rebecca pushed Kyle aside. 'Sven, what are you doing? Are you crazy?'

'Not so crazy, I think.' Jörgensen had produced a length of electrical wire from the bag. 'Actually, at the moment I'm pretty happy with the way things are going. Turn towards the wall, please.'

Kyle felt his hands being bound tightly together, the wire snaking around his body, anchoring him to the metal banister that ran around the ballroom's perimeter. The process was repeated for Rebecca, leaving them standing side by side, bound to the building's fabric.

'I can't bring myself to shoot you,' Jörgensen stood beside her and took Rebecca's chin in his hand. 'Not after you've been so useful. So *obliging*.'

Rebecca shook him off. 'I hope you enjoy prison, Sven, because that's where you'll be spending the rest of your miserable life.'

'I think not,' Sven chuckled. 'Not after what Mr Munday has told me about the joys of incarceration. No, my preference is for ... warmer climes.' He tested the wire, checked that it was tight all the way around. Kyle tried to keep his muscles flexed, but the Swede had done a thorough job. Jörgensen stood back to examine his handiwork.

'I hope you will forgive me for a rather dramatic gesture, but I thought it might appeal to you both.'

'What are you going to do, Sven?' Rebecca didn't sound scared, just furious.

'As I said, a little dramatic, perhaps, but I can't resist.'

His footsteps receded into the centre of the ballroom. Then came three loud gunshots.

For a few moments nothing happened. 'Take steady, deep breaths,' Kyle whispered, 'to oxygenate your body.' As he spoke, an agonised groan of weary metalwork rang out across the ballroom as the water pressure sought out the new weakness in the structure.

'You should have some moments to say goodbye, with a

little luck,' Jörgensen shouted. 'I apologise that I have to leave you.'

They heard him break into a run as he made for the connecting tunnel, firing one last shot for good measure. This time there was an immediate response from the ballroom's opposite end, the sound of rushing water.

The creaking above them intensified. Kyle turned his eyes upwards, searching for the damage. Just off centre, a crack was spreading across the roof. At that moment he was more worried about falling glass than water, but at the edge of the room they should escape the worst of any falling debris. He worked his hands against the wire but Jörgensen had done his job with typical Nordic efficiency.

Rebecca met his gaze in silent comprehension.

With a final roar like a clap of thunder, the lake crashed down onto their heads.

Chapter Twelve

The water level was rising faster than Kyle could think. He reckoned they had four, maybe five minutes before they were submerged. Rebecca was already shaking with cold, and the harder he tugged at the wire, the tighter it gripped his wrists.

'Underneath.' Rebecca had moved her hand beneath the rail, was running her fingers along it. 'There's a rough edge.' She began to move her wrists from side to side, scraping the wire that looped from her wrists along the rail's rough, serrated edge.

Kyle checked. She was right; instead of sealing the railing, the builders had cut corners, left the metalwork unfinished. But how thick was the wire's core? The old metalwork might cut through the plastic but would it be robust enough to sever the wire itself? Kyle applied himself to the task, sawing at the short length that looped from his wrists around the rail.

The water was up to their waists; they had three minutes at most. Kyle sawed harder. His head was pounding, and he could feel his heart working overtime. This wasn't good for him, but then drowning was hardly a better option.

Rebecca was frantically working her hands back and forth, her lips blue, teeth chattering. The roof was making an ominous noise, different than before; now it groaned with an unearthly sound that put Kyle in mind of an earthquake he had once experienced in Sicily when the building he was in had begun to collapse. He remembered ducking instinctively, dashing for the exit with his hands covering his head. A minute later the whole building had come down.

The water level was still rising. Soon it would reach Rebecca's shoulders. Kyle recalculated. A minute and a half at best. He redoubled his efforts.

The wire wouldn't give.

'The automatic,' Rebecca yelled. 'He dropped it. It must be somewhere nearby.'

Kyle ducked his head under the freezing water. It was murky, he couldn't see a thing. He strained his eyes, looking for a small, dark shape. A needle in a haystack would be easier to spot. He stretched his feet, tugged the wire for maximum extension, moved his legs in a wide arc.

Nothing.

He kicked off his shoes, tried again. Something touched his toe. It could be anything, a piece of ceiling debris, or… He tried to get his foot on top of the object, but only succeeded in nudging it further away. Rebecca was breathing hard, the water up to her chin.

He wanted to hold her, tell her how he felt about her. He did the next best thing, rested his wrists gently against her cheek. 'Take deep breaths, *really* slow.'

Kyle pulled hard on the wire, straining for an extra centimetre between his wrists. It gave a little. He tried again, ignoring the pain shooting through his tendons. He gained another centimetre and with it a little more freedom of movement. He carried on until he had created enough slack to be confident of being able to use his fingers. He brushed his foot along the floor, searching for the object. Again, nothing. Whatever it was had moved away, propelled by the movement of the water.

'Cam, I'm sorry I dragged you into this.' Rebecca's lips were only just above the water. Her eyes met his. 'I'm sorry I hurt you.'

'You can give me the unabridged version later,' Kyle said. He swept his feet across the floor again. This time his right foot connected with something hard. He covered it with his whole foot, pulled it towards him. The shape felt right. When he was sure he could bend and retrieve it he removed his foot. He ducked, made a grab for it. It almost slipped away in the artificial current but then his fingers snagged around a circular projection and he felt a burst of elation knowing that he'd grabbed the automatic by its trigger guard. He resurfaced, shook the water from it.

Rebecca had disappeared; only the top of her head was visible. Kyle muttered a prayer, grabbed Rebecca's wrists. There was a little clearance; trying not to worry about ricochet or the proximity of the automatic to her flesh, he placed the muzzle against the wire and pulled the trigger. The gun went off and he felt Rebecca's wrists separate. He helped her as best he could to unwind the loose wire; her head broke the surface and she drew in a huge whoop of air. She took the gun from him and repeated the process to free his own hands.

'Can you swim?'

'As it happens, yes,' Rebecca replied. 'Hundred metres junior champion, St Helen's School, summer of fifty-seven.'

'Sorry I asked.'

'I'll tell you about the water polo later.'

Keeping to the ballroom's edge, they struck out towards

the entrance tunnel. Kyle was trying to remember how far he'd walked along it with Jörgensen earlier. And what about the stairs? The length of time they'd have to hold their breaths would depend on how high the water had risen.

Kyle estimated that by the time they'd swum along the tunnel, assuming no obstructions, they'd still have to swim up to almost the top of the stairwell, again assuming no obstructions, before their heads broke water. That meant holding their breath for at least two minutes, maybe longer. He thought he could manage it, although it wasn't something he practised regularly. But could Rebecca?

At the approximate spot they began to tread water. The distance between them and the ceiling was closing rapidly as the water level continued to rise but Kyle didn't want to rely on their being able to escape through the broken glass into the body of the lake; too many unknowns. Rebecca was casting worried glances at the ceiling

'Back in a sec.'

He duck-dived to check their position and was immediately concerned at the depth – the floor was at least fifteen feet below. He kicked out for the hazy shape of the tunnel, and swam a good ten metres into its interior. He made out a lighter shade of green ahead – the stairwell. It seemed further away than he remembered, but at least the route was unobstructed.

He quickly made his way back, his lungs aching for air, and broke the surface beside Rebecca. He took a moment to recover. Rebecca was looking at him anxiously. Her lips were even bluer than before, her pupils dilated. Kyle recognised the symptoms of shock and wondered if he looked the same.

'Ready for this?' He dragged the corners of his mouth into

a smile.

'Oh, yeah,' Rebecca nodded. 'Bring it on.'

This time Kyle's grin was spontaneous. 'Good. So ... deep breaths for thirty seconds, one huge breath, then down we go.'

Chapter Thirteen

The second time was harder – much harder. Twenty seconds into the tunnel and Kyle was struggling for air. Rebecca was keeping pace with him, pulling herself along with wide, confident strokes. His heart was banging in his chest and the distant stairwell wasn't getting closer quickly enough.

They reached a narrowing Kyle remembered from earlier – it seemed a lifetime ago – where a gate had once barred the entrance to the ballroom. All that remained were the rusted hinges, sharp projections from the peeling plaster walls of the tunnel – and it was one of these that caught his shirtsleeve. The heavy cotton snagged around the hinge and wasn't letting go. Rebecca was forging ahead, unaware of his predicament, while he was using too much oxygen – oxygen he couldn't afford to lose. His lungs were on fire.

Rebecca turned, saw what had happened. He shook his head, not wanting her to put herself at risk, but she swam to his side, nimble fingers working down his shirt buttons. He shrugged the garment off, fixed his eyes on the dim luminescence ahead. He wasn't going to make it. He needed to take a breath, not in a few seconds, but *now*.

He felt Rebecca grab him under the armpit, bully him along the final section of tunnel. Now they were at the base of the stairwell. Kyle angled his body up, straining for the surface. He could see it, tantalisingly close, just a few feet above. His chest was a band of agony. He had to take a breath or he would die.

Kyle's vision fogged and he felt his limbs slacken; his brain was closing down. For a mad moment he wondered if he might be able to breathe like a fish, a fleeting, primeval instinct, just one lungful would be enough, just so he could feed his body the air it craved...

His head broke the surface and he felt himself being pulled from the water, spread out flat on the rough, uneven ground of the stairwell entrance. He lay spreadeagled, gasping like a landed fish, chest heaving, heart palpitating. Someone was talking to him but it could have been anyone, anything. Gradually, the words began to take shape, make some kind of sense. He caught the end of the last sentence and groaned with relief.

'...haven't had so much fun since my sports coach got us to try synchronised swimming. It was a mess, I can tell you. We all nearly drowned.'

Kyle heard himself laugh, but was it really him, or someone else? It was too difficult to work out. He shut his eyes and darkness closed in. He imagined himself afloat on a raft in the middle of a calm, flat sea. All was still. The unbroken line of the horizon was the only mark of topography, a flat boundary between sea and sky. The water stretched for miles in every direction and he was alone. Kyle felt the raft bob gently beneath him. Alone was just fine; it didn't bother him at all.

He was the only person left alive in a world of endless water.

'Cameron? Can you hear me?'

The voice was annoyingly persistent. It wouldn't stop. Couldn't they understand that he just wanted to sleep?

'*Cameron!*'

His eyes shot open. Everything was wrong. Too bright, too loud.

'Welcome back.'

He moved his head experimentally to the right, towards the source of the sound. 'Rebecca.'

'Well, that's a good sign.'

'What is?' Kyle squinted. His head hurt – a score of between six and seven on the HSD.

She squeezed his arm. 'You know me, that's what.'

Kyle tried to make sense of the words. Failed.

'Cam, listen…'

Her voice was gentler. That was worrying. That meant she was about to reveal something, probably something bad.

'Cam, you've been out cold for a good couple of hours. I thought you might not … I mean, we thought there was a chance that…'

Now he was fully awake. 'Are you kidding me?' He tried to sit up, but was restrained by … what? Tubes, things on his arm attached to bleeping monitors.

Not again…

He gave up, flopped his head onto the pillow and then his memory kicked in with a blast. The ballroom, the water. *Jörgensen…*

He shifted on the pillows, tried to swing his legs out of bed.

'*Cameron!* What are you *doing?*'

'Can't stay. I've an urgent appointment with your boyfriend. I'm going to break his arms and hang him up by his scrotum.'

'Cameron, *no!* You're not well enough. You have to leave Sven to the police.'

Now Kyle's head was a pounding drum. 'Leave it? Are you serious? He tried to kill us.'

'I know, but–'

'I have to find him. Patterson won't get close. He'll be looking in all the wrong places; trust me, the guy's a serial procrastinator. Ticks all the boxes except the one that says "result".'

'Cameron, you almost died. You were lucky. When I pulled you out of the water I thought I'd lost you. The doctor said your body couldn't cope with that level of physical strain so soon after your previous injury. Your heart nearly gave out.'

Kyle eased his legs over the side of the bed a second time.

'Cam, this is a really bad idea. You need rest.'

'And I intend to see that he gets it.' A uniformed nurse had appeared at the foot of the bed, carrying a syringe on a tray. 'Now, if you please, Mr Kyle.'

Kyle had managed to sit up, but his head was swimming. He felt disoriented, as though his conversation with Rebecca had taken place solely in his imagination. Firm hands pressed him back onto the bed and, moments later, a sharp sting in his arm put an end to his self-discharge ambitions. His eyelids grew heavy, and before long he was back on his solitary raft, only this time he was travelling at a sedate speed along a wide, endless canal, the walls of which stretched high on either side like the jaws of some ancient sea monster.

He slept soundly in the mouth of the beast.

Chapter Fourteen

Kyle awoke with a start.. The window was a black rectangle and his side ward was bathed in muted, bluish light. He felt a little groggy, but otherwise all right. Furtive figures moved around within earshot, the sound of soft soles on polished floors interspersed with brief, monosyllabic conversations. The subdued sounds of a hospital at night.

What was the time? Come to that, what day was it?

The sparsely furnished room offered no clues but to Kyle it felt like three in the morning, the wee, small hours. Night staff, little activity.

Perfect.

He sat up, pleased to note that his tubes had been removed. Nothing but his own body bound him to the steel hospital frame, and when he planted his feet on the sheet vinyl floor and stood up his head remained reassuringly level and the local horizon stayed where it was.

On the bedside cabinet next to a plastic pitcher of water and a paper cup, there was an envelope bearing his name neatly written in red felt tip pen. Kyle picked it up, ripped it open.

Cam,

Don't be angry, but I've gone to look for Sven. Please don't worry –

I'm sure he won't hurt me. I just want to talk to him. I need answers – you can understand that, I'm sure. Keep safe and take it easy. I'll be in touch soon, I promise.

R x

PS I didn't call the police – and they still don't know where I am. I took the automatic, too. Didn't want anyone asking any awkward questions. Hope you're OK. R.

Kyle swore. It was just the crazy kind of thing Bec would do. Jörgensen had tried to kill them both, and they'd witnessed him dispose of a colleague – or hired hand – without a second thought. What did she expect to happen if and when she succeeded in tracking him down? A frank exchange of views, some kind of reconciliation? Hardly; Jörgensen would shoot her out of hand.

But that was Bec all over. Determined, stubborn, yet soft-centred and always ready to see the best in people. There was no 'best' to see in Jörgensen. The guy was a certifiable criminal, as bad as – or possibly even worse than – Munday.

Kyle's clothes were neatly folded over the radiator. He took an experimental step and found that forward movement was not only possible, but pain-free. He dressed quickly. His clothing was still a little damp but the risk of catching a chill scarcely registered on the life-threatening scale compared to their narrow escape from the ballroom. He checked his jacket pocket. Here was his wallet, his keys; in short, everything he required. Muttering a prayer of thanks and sending a telepathic hug to Bec, he quickly dressed and went to the doorway.

Wait.

His notes were attached to the end of the bed, conveniently placed for medical staff to access. He quickly checked the contents. Admission, nine pm. Arrival in ward, ten twelve pm. A note: briefly conscious at eleven seventeen. DZP: 10mg.

Diazepam. No wonder he felt groggy. The last entry was an hourly check. All the hours were ticked up to and including four am.

The side ward opened into a corridor. To his left, the nurses' station. To his right, the exit.

A rapid series of beeps and buzzes mobilised a trio of nursing staff. Kyle watched as they abandoned the nurses' station and hurried off to another part of the ward. He took his opportunity and slipped out of the side room. Seconds later he was at the exit. The wall clock above the door read four fifty-two. He pushed, half expecting it to be locked, but it swung open freely.

Now he was in a wider corridor, one of the main hospital arteries. He kept moving, passing white-coated doctors rushing to some emergency, a cleaner moving a wide brush to and fro across the vinyl floor with studied boredom, a distraught woman being comforted by a younger man, until he eventually arrived at the hospital's main entrance.

At that point he realised he had no idea which town he was in. The night attendant at the reception desk was looking at him with a quizzical expression. Feeling a little foolish, he greeted the man with a cheery smile.

'Morning. I wonder if you can help me?'

'Of course, sir.'

'Where exactly is this hospital located?'

'Where? You mean whereabouts in Romford?'

'Romford? Ah, right. You see, I was brought in unconscious.'

'We're on the west side of town, sir, not far from the station.'

'I see. That's helpful. Thank you – a train is what I'm after.' Kyle started to walk away.

'You won't find many leaving at this time of day,' the man called after him.

Kyle raised his arm to acknowledge the observation. He just wanted to get out before a posse of nurses from his ward came looking for him.

'Are you sure you're well enough, sir?'

Kyle kept walking.

Outside the air was mild and a light drizzle was falling. Romford; he hadn't been here for a long, long time. The mainline station connected directly to Liverpool Street, and from there a short train or bus ride would take him to Clapton. He could catch an early train, but right now he just needed to walk, clear his head, think.

The drizzle intensified and he lengthened his stride, swung left towards the station. Maybe there'd be a Lyons open. At worst he'd be able to get under cover, wait for the first train to Liverpool Street.

A car drew up behind him. He half-turned, anticipating a taxi, but a Romford cabby's vehicle of choice was unlikely to be a Mini Cooper. The guy probably wanted directions. Kyle bent to the lowering window as the driver leaned across the passenger seat.

'Get in.'

A silenced pistol was balanced in the crook of the driver's

arm. Kyle recognised him straight away.

'I said, *get in*.'

Kyle stole a glance up and down the road, but there were no cruising patrol cars to come to his aid, just an empty milk float and an out-of-service bus that sloshed past with an impatient honk of its horn.

Kyle got in.

The Mini moved off. The pistol in the driver's gloved hand was steady, and pointing in his direction.

'Fasten your seat belt, please.'

Kyle fastened his seat belt. It wouldn't be wise to argue with a man like Kenneth Munday.

Chapter Fifteen

'Thought you might be able to help me out,' Munday said. 'Help me find somebody.'

'You're way past the stage of needing a lawyer.'

'Very funny, Mr Kyle.' Munday steered the Mini into Victoria Road. 'So you know exactly who I'm talking about.' His voice was low, gravelly – the voice of a man not used to much conversation. 'What else do you know?'

'I know the entire country is looking for you.'

'Well that makes you the cleverest ex-copper in England then, doesn't it? Seeing as how you've found me all by yourself.' Munday chuckled.

Kyle watched the man from the corner of his eye. It was hard not to when there was a pistol pointed in your direction. Munday was in his late forties, well-built, sporting what Bec would describe as an American hair cut – cropped to a length of about a centimetre. His complexion was waxy and unhealthy-looking – the inevitable result, Kyle supposed, of infrequent exposure to natural light. The fugitive was clean shaven with hooded, watchful eyes and a nose that looked as if it had been broken on several occasions. Kyle found himself wondering how Munday's opponents had fared in the scraps, but then he remembered the two convicts Munday had managed to entice into his cell.

'Bit risky, driving around this time of the morning,' Kyle

said. 'Unless you want to be caught, of course.'

'Let's get one thing straight, Mr Kyle. I don't have a risk-averse personality. If you want to get ahead, risks are par for the course.'

Bec's assessment of Munday had been spot on. The guy seemed intelligent, his choice of vocabulary not what you might expect from a violent lifer. But Kyle needed answers.

'OK, here's a question. Your mate Jörgensen tried to kill me – and Rebecca. Your idea?'

'Ah, Rebecca.' Munday turned left at the Drill roundabout towards Gidea Park station. 'Nice kid. We've had some … interesting discussions.'

'You used her.'

'She told me a lot about you.' Now they were crawling along a suburban street. Munday found a space and pulled over. 'Out you get.' He gestured with the pistol.

'Where are we going?'

'Far too many questions,' Munday said.

'One more, if I may?'

Munday looked at Kyle. 'That was one of the things she told me.'

'What?'

'That you could be a pain in the neck.'

'Indulge me. How did you know where I was?'

Munday narrowed his eyes. 'Let's just say I had a strong suspicion that something had gone awry. If you know point A, it's straightforward enough to track back and figure out point B, the hospital that might be first port of call for an emergency ambulance.'

'I'm betting there's more than just the lake stash to pick up. Jörgensen was on collection duty, wasn't he? But he failed to return to base. Am I right?'

'Didn't have you down as a betting man, Mr Kyle. Out.'

This time Munday jammed the pistol into Kyle's ribs. Kyle got out.

The rain was still falling in a dismal, early morning patter. Munday walked behind him and directed him to a house with a prominent *For Sale* sign displayed in the front garden. Kyle heard keys rattling, and Munday's hand reached past him and unlocked the front door.

'Inside.'

The house smelled of desertion, the stale scent of old newspapers mingled with a hint of rising damp. Munday prodded Kyle into the living room and opened the curtains. Pale dawn light filtered in through grimy windows, revealing only two pieces of furniture; a sofa and an armchair. Munday sat in the latter, gestured with the gun for Kyle to sit opposite.

'This is cozy,' Kyle said. 'Not sure about the wallpaper, though. I'd have gone for something plainer–'

'Enough. I'll get to the point. You're right. Jörgensen's double-crossed me. But nobody does that and gets away with it. You weren't something I'd factored in, Mr Kyle, but you could turn out to be useful enough, provided we can come to an agreement.'

'An agreement? You're an on-the-run prisoner with a price on your head. You'll be back in Fairview in days. Hours, even.'

'I don't think so, Mr Kyle.' Munday leaned forward. 'Look, I'll confide in you; I *am* a betting man, as it happens. And I'd put money on you wanting to ensure Rebecca's safety. So, how about this: you know how the police work, so you can be my ears and eyes. You help me find Jörgensen, and I'll make sure the lovely Rebecca comes to no harm. Deal?'

'Since you put it like that, it looks like I have very little choice.'

'Good. I'm glad we see eye-to-eye.' Munday got up and went to the window, peered out, scanned the road. He turned to face the room. 'You'll be aware, Mr Kyle, that I have friends – a good number of friends – all able and willing to carry out any tasks I might care to allocate. If anything untoward should happen to me, they have instructions as to how to proceed. Get my drift?'

'Very clearly.'

'Good. So I suggest we put any ill-feeling aside for the time being,' Munday tucked the gun into his coat pocket, 'and put our heads together, as it were, to try to establish a way forward.'

Munday sat down again. 'So, our friend Jörgensen. Where is he? What's his next move? To my mind, it's very simple. There are two clear possibilities. One is Southend-on-Sea, the other a little closer.'

Kyle nodded. 'Your remaining repositories, I assume.' He considered the options. Jörgensen seemed like a cut-to-the-chase kind of bloke. The guy was based in London, so it made sense to start wide, then come back in. He said, 'My money's on Southend as his first port of call.'

'Excellent. I agree. I think we'll work well together.'

'I'll think a lot better on a full stomach.'

Munday laughed, a jarringly normal sound. 'There's a Lyons café just around the corner. Why don't you pop out and procure some breakfast? We can eat on the way.'

Chapter Sixteen

'He has a few hours on us,' Kyle said to Munday as the Mini lurched to a standstill at a set of pedestrian lights. There was a small parade of shops to their left.

'Doesn't matter. He'll have to wait till the place opens.' Munday revved the engine. 'Come *on*.' He drummed his fingers on the steering wheel as an elderly woman shuffled slowly across the road.

'Easy,' Kyle said. 'She's eighty if she's a day. And what do you mean, wait till it opens? Don't tell me you've stashed your loot in a shop?'

'Not exactly,' Munday said. 'You'll see.'

A greengrocer's caught Kyle's eye. 'Hold on.'

Munday shot him an angry look.

'Should've stashed it in a greengrocer's – always open bright and early.' Kyle got out before Munday could object.

Kyle entered the shop and quickly made a purchase.

Munday had moved to a bus stop a few yards beyond the pedestrian crossing. As Kyle opened the passenger door, Munday growled at him, 'Gentle warning. We may be partners for now, but don't do that again. What's in the bag?'

Kyle rummaged and retrieved an orange. 'Just fancied one. Want a bit?' He began to peel the fruit with a penknife.

'No, I do not.' Munday swung the car into the traffic and they continued their journey in silence for the next quarter of an hour.

As they joined the Southend Arterial Road, Munday cleared his throat and shot Kyle a glance. 'You all right? Fitness-wise, I mean? And I'm not talking about the lake.'

'Never felt better.' Kyle tore off another orange segment. 'Why? What's Rebecca been telling you?'

'That you were shot. That you were out cold for weeks.' Another sideways glance. 'And that you were lucky. Or maybe you had good doctors – or maybe it was a bit of both.'

'Doctors, neuro-consultants, psychologists.' Kyle spat a pip into his hand. 'You name it, I had them.'

Munday guffawed. 'Psychologists?'

'Yep. Long story short, they told me I'm borderline psychotic. But don't worry, it'll most likely pass.'

'You serious?' Munday shifted in his seat.

'Deadly. By the way, who was the guy at the lake?'

Munday shook his head. 'An amateur, as it turned out.'

'I've formed the impression that things didn't turn out as expected.'

'You could say that.'

'I'm all ears.'

Munday floored the accelerator and the Mini shot forward. 'It can wait.'

Kyle changed the subject. 'DI Patterson was your arresting officer, wasn't he? Way back when.'

'So?'

'He'll be highly motivated to track you down, that's all I was thinking.'

'Patterson was a Sergeant at the time,' Munday corrected him. 'And frankly, I don't give a toss about his motivation. He ain't going to find me.'

The A127 was busy with morning traffic. A police car with flashing lights passed them on the opposite carriageway but Munday seemed unperturbed. Kyle turned on the radio. Andy Williams' soft croon filled the small car. *You're just too good to be true. Can't take my eyes off you...* Kyle closed his eyes and thought of Rebecca. He just needed to know she was safe. That would be enough.

The song ended and the DJ rattled off a few inane comments before spinning another disc. This time it was Engelbert: *Lonely is a man without love* ... Kyle reached down and switched the radio off.

'I was listening to that,' Munday growled.

'Engelbert's old hat. Sergeant Pepper or Hendrix is where it's at these days.'

'If you say so.'

Kyle realised that Munday had probably never heard of either, having been in solitary until comparatively recently. It was a sober reminder that he was sitting in a car with a convicted murderer.

Forty-five minutes later they were crawling through traffic towards Southend's main promenade. Kyle caught occasional glimpses of the sea between the nondescript housing, a flat grey expanse lurking beyond the town like a restless storm cloud.

Munday cruised slowly along the front. Southend's famous pier loomed long and wave-lashed to their right alongside an amusement park proclaiming itself as *Peter Pan's Playground,* which Kyle had vague memories of having visited as a child.

Munday found a space and parked. 'See that?' Munday pointed to the amusement park entrance. 'In there you'll find

The Crooked House. Inside, on the first floor there's a room of mirrors. A bench runs all the way around it. In the corner, there's a lever just under the lip of the bench. You'll feel it with your fingers. It's well recessed, but just run your hand along and you'll find it. Open it up. There's a box inside. Bring the box.'

Kyle looked across at the amusement park. It was open, but there were only a few folk moving around within its perimeter – employees rather than punters at this hour of the day. He imagined that trade would pick up later in the morning – it was a Saturday, after all.

'We wait,' Munday said, as if reading his thoughts, 'or you'll stick out like a sore thumb.'

They waited. An hour passed, and the park gradually filled up with families and excitable children.

'That'll do,' Munday announced. 'In you go.'

'Do I pay to get in?'

'Don't ask stupid questions. Just bring me what's in the box.'

Kyle shrugged. 'Don't talk to any policemen while I'm away.'

He got out and shut the door on Munday's expletive.

Chapter Seventeen

Kyle stood on the pavement outside *Peter Pan's Playground*. Above the arched entrance, a mechanical Popeye rocked back and forth in a rowing boat tossed by imaginary waves. Kyle joined the queue for the ticket office, wincing at the shrill racket made by children behind and in front of him. Five minutes later he reached the front of the queue. A red-faced woman wearing fingerless gloves and a drab raincoat greeted him with a puff of cigarette smoke.

'Yes, love. How many can I do you for?'

'One adult, please.'

She looked at him and winked. 'Young at heart, eh?'

Kyle paid and pocketed the ticket. More and more families were arriving, along with groups of young lads and huddles of giggling teenage girls, and the queue now snaked back a fair distance along the promenade pavement. Kyle stood to one side and surveyed the scene.

The rain had cleared and the sun washed the park in a sparkling brightness that hurt his eyes. The grounds were dominated by the garish yellow and red of the tall helter-skelter. Kyle squinted and scanned the park for the *Crooked House* attraction that Munday had described. Yellow and red seemed to be the dominant colour, most of the attractions having followed the helter-skelter's vibrant colour scheme – apart from the *Crooked House*, which was a whitewashed jumble of displaced angles and twisted window frames.

Kyle made a beeline for the woman in the Crooked House's ticket booth. She looked up as he approached 'All right, darlin'? One to go? 'Ere you are, my lovely.' The woman looked him up and down. 'Bless me if I'm not even sure you're going to fit in the 'ouse at all.'

'I'll manage.' Kyle snatched the proffered ticket, suddenly fearful that she – or the tattooed bloke busy with some maintenance task by the turnstile – might try to stop him.

'One coming through, Steve,' she yelled.

But Steve just gave him a flat-eyed stare, swung the turnstile open and let him pass.

Kyle ducked his head under the low door beam and went in.

He eased himself through narrow, claustrophobic passages, passing weird, glass-fronted dioramas as he went – the Mad Hatter's tea party, a Scrooge-like character in bed, a workshop inhabited by dwarfs oddly missing their Snow White – and climbed a flight of uneven stairs to arrive in a room with a canted floor and walls that reflected his arrival as a bizarrely distorted version of himself, excessively tall one moment and then compressed to a short, ball-like character with stumpy legs.

Kyle slid across the room and sat awkwardly on the wooden bench, polished to a shine by a thousand or more pairs of buttocks. Raised, over-excited voices and gales of laughter floated up from downstairs; he wouldn't be in the room alone for long. The piped music, a loud, tinny assortment of nursery rhymes and children's songs, was beginning to grate on his nerves.

He ran his fingers beneath the seating, searching for the

lever that Munday had described. He'd said it was in a corner, but which? Kyle slid along the bench to the opposite side. Now he felt it: a ridge of raised woodwork set into the edge just below the seat. He pulled, pressed. Nothing. He slid it to one side. Something clicked. He bent to inspect the result. A small door had sprung open. He reached his hand into the hollow, vaguely aware that the house had fallen silent. The laughter and noise below had stopped and the music had cut off mid-phrase.

He quickly felt around in the gap. There was a small, moveable object; he pulled it out. It was a box, fourteen or fifteen inches wide, maybe ten inches deep. He opened it. There was a slip of paper, nothing else. He withdrew it, unfolded it. In scrawled biro, a message:

Cam, if you're here, please leave quickly. Don't get involved in this. Sorry. R x

Baffled, Kyle pocketed the message and shut the lid. He tucked the box under his arm and looked for the exit corridor.

'Oi,' a voice growled behind him. 'You with that bird from earlier?'

Kyle turned, only to receive a heavy fist that smashed into his cheekbone with a loud, shocking *crunch*. He reeled, dropped the box, which skittered away across the sloping floor. He scrambled to his feet to see Steve, the guy from the turnstile, squaring up to him, fists raised like a Victorian pugilist. His arms were blue with naval tattoos and a long scar ran the length of his forehead, dipping down over one eyebrow to form a fleshy exclamation mark.

'Big guy on his own. Up to no good, I said to Marge. Thievin', I'll bet. Now, you gonna answer my question? You with that bird? Where'd she go, eh?'

Kyle bent and retrieved the box, held it at arm's length. 'Here you go.'

The man dropped his fists. 'No fight in yer, eh?'

Kyle grinned, shrugged. 'It's OK, Steve. There's no problem here.' He watched for the telltale changes in his assailant's body language that would signal the right moment. Just a little more ... a little more...

Now...

The moment Steve's hands touched the box Kyle snatched it away, swung it around and brought it crashing down on his head, knocking him sideways against the mirrored wall. The big man's fists came up again, but this time Kyle was ready. He smashed his own firmly bunched hand into Steve's nose.

Blood sprayed across the mirrors and Steve howled, put his head down and charged at Kyle like a bull. Kyle sidestepped and his opponent's impetus took him past Kyle, past the bench, and into the gap at the edge of the room that led directly into the exit stairwell. Kyle heard the thundering descent as Steve's body bounced on the uneven steps until, with a final crash, it came to rest. Kyle followed, taking care to negotiate the steps one at a time, stepped over the prone body and into the daylight.

He walked quickly away from the *Crooked House* with the box tucked under his arm, craning his neck above the bustling crowds for a glimpse of Rebecca. *That bird...*

'Hey, mister!'

Two small boys ran up to him, their faces shining with expectation.

'It *is* the box,' the smaller boy said to the other. 'Same markings.'

'Can I help?' Kyle frowned.

'A lady said she'd give us ten bob if we came in with her,' the little one said. He was wearing grey shorts and a yellow shirt, the front of which bore stains from a recently consumed ice cream. 'But she went off with this bloke,' the taller one chipped in. 'She never gave us nothing.'

'Ten bob?' Kyle reached into his pocket and took out half a crown. 'I can't manage ten bob, but here's something for you, anyway.' He held it out, but as the smaller boy went to grab it he closed his fist over the coin. 'Uh uh.' He shook his head. 'You've got to earn it.'

The taller boy made a face and looked at his mate. 'Like, how?'

'When did the lady take you into the Crooked House?'

''Bout half an hour ago,' the taller boy said. 'Then she just went off with this bloke. He wasn't very nice,' he added.

'Wasn't much in the box anyway,' the little one said.

'I'm guessing the lady gave something to the man? Whatever was in the box?' Kyle prompted.

'Yeah.' The little one looked at his shoes. 'I reckon he was hurting her. He grabbed her arm like this.' He demonstrated by clutching his friend's arm, who gave a howl of protest. '*Ow*, get off Jim! That bloody 'urt.'

'Hey, language.' Kyle affected a stern expression. 'Do you remember which way they went?'

'She give 'im something – looked like a key or summink, then they just left,' Jim said. 'I see 'em on the pavement thru the fence, didn't I?'

'Did you see them get into a car?'

'Naw. He wanted to go on the dipper, didn't 'e?' Jim scowled at his mate. 'But they wouldn't let us anyhow. Said we needed an adult wiv us.'

'Come on, then,' Kyle said. 'I'll sign you in.'

He gave them the half-crown and escorted them to the big dipper, paid at the kiosk and left them in a state of nervous excitement. 'Fanks, mister,' Jim called over his shoulder. 'You're the best!'

Kyle headed for the exit, skirting cautiously around the *Crooked House*, but there was no sign of his attacker. The music had recommenced and people were going in and coming out, so he assumed that the tattooed man was nursing his wounds somewhere else.

While he'd been in the playground the promenade had grown into a bustling freeway. Kyle looked for a gold XJ6, but there was only the usual suburban mix of Cortinas, family estates and open-topped buses streaming to and fro along the front.

Kyle threaded his way through the crowds towards the solitary Mini, just a few hundred yards up the prom from where Munday had originally parked it. As he drew closer he noticed that the door was slightly open. By the time he reached it he already knew what he'd find. Sure enough, the Mini was empty.

The keys were in the ignition, but Munday had gone.

Chapter Eighteen

Kyle drove slowly along the A127. He had no license, no insurance but that was just tough; Munday had dumped the Mini, Kyle needed transport, and he was in no mood to hang around train stations.

His headache had returned with a vengeance. He tried to empty his mind, give his brain some respite, but the thought of Rebecca going anywhere near the seriously unstable Jörgensen kept the grey matter ticking like a time bomb. Where was she? Where had Munday gone? He theorised that Munday had caught sight of either Rebecca or Jörgensen outside the amusement park and decided to follow them. But on foot? It made no sense. He supposed Munday might have hot-wired another car, but why bother? The Mini was unassuming enough. Of course, there was always the chance that the fugitive had been spotted and arrested by some alert bobby on the beat, but Kyle dismissed that possibility; Munday would never allow himself to be recaptured so easily. No, the lifer was still at large, and for some reason he had decided to dispense with his short-term partner.

By the time Kyle parked the Mini outside his flat he was no further forward in his suppositions. He needed a bath, something to eat, and a pot of strong tea, not necessarily in that order. He took the stairs two at a time and arrived breathless on the landing. As he approached his front door, however, it opened. He took a step back in surprise.

DC Bates looked as startled as he felt. Her face was chalky and her hand, when she raised it either in greeting or instinctive self-defence, was trembling. Kyle recognised the classic symptoms of shock.

'DC Kyle – I – there's been a ... an incident. I must ask you to wait here while I call for assistance.' She slipped her hand into her pocket, not, Kyle thought, to retrieve a weapon, but rather to hide her tremor.

'*Ex*-DC Kyle, he corrected her. 'What's happened? What are you doing in my flat?'

Bates' face drained of blood. Kyle realised that she was about to faint so he stepped forward just in time to catch her as she pitched forward into his arms. He managed to manoeuvre her into the lounge with the intention of laying her on the settee, but the settee was already occupied.

DI Patterson was sitting bolt upright, his face even paler than Bates', but there was a good reason for that, and it wasn't shock; Patterson was stone dead, Kyle's silver letter opener embedded in the back of his neck. His shirt and jacket were soaked in blood, as was the settee and a wide area of carpet.

Kyle did an about-turn, made a beeline for the bedroom. A little inappropriate, but Bates was still out cold and there was nowhere else to lie her down comfortably. She moaned softly as he laid her gently on the counterpane. He went through to the kitchen, poured a small measure of Metaxa, clicked on the kettle as he passed it on his way back.

Bates was stirring, her cheeks regaining some of their lost colour. Kyle set the brandy glass down on his bedside table.

'Feeling better?' He picked up the tumbler and held it under her nose. Bates grasped the glass, took a sip, coughed and sat up. '*What* is *that?*'

'Metaxa,' Kyle told her. 'Greek rocket fuel. Friend of mine brought me a bottle from Crete last year.'

'It's disgusting.' Bates coughed again, made a face.

'It does the job.' Kyle took the glass and set it down. 'So, tell me, what happened?'

Bates seemed to suddenly remember where she was. Her face fell. 'He was a ... a right bastard, but he didn't deserve that.' She looked at Kyle for confirmation.

'He was, and he didn't,' Kyle agreed. 'And you're going to tell me you found him like that.'

'Yes. He said he was going to search your flat properly – as if the fingerprint team hadn't done that already.'

'And then he didn't show up back at the ranch?'

Bates took a breath. 'Yes. This morning he was supposed to be at the ten o'clock briefing.'

'OK.' Kyle offered the glass a second time but Bates declined. A strand of auburn hair had come loose; it trailed down her cheek to her chest and Kyle had a job not to follow it with his eyes. 'I take it I'm not a suspect?'

'You?' She looked him up and down and her expression shifted, as though she hadn't considered that possibility. After a moment she said, 'No. But I do want to know where you've been. *And* what you've been doing.' She sat up, swung her legs over the edge of the bed, brushed herself down.

'Long story,' Kyle said. 'First you'd better telephone this in.'

'Yes.' Bates gathered herself. 'Of course.'

'If you're sure you're all right. I'll have a sniff around in the meantime.'

Bates winced. 'I'll be fine as long as you don't give me any more of that disgusting potion. And *don't* touch anything.'

She shot him a stern look.

'I'm an ex-DC, remember? My mental faculties may be compromised, but I'm not completely daft.'

'Of course. Sorry.' Bates hurried out of the flat, averting her eyes, Kyle noticed, from the half-open door of the lounge.

Kyle ran through a list of perpetrators as he spooned tea into the pot. It was a short list. Two candidates fitted the profile: one, Jörgensen, and two, Munday. But why would either of them want Patterson dead? The DI would be replaced and the pursuit would continue, so killing the detective would give Munday no advantage, except perhaps some satisfaction at having settled an old score. Besides, Kyle was sure that Munday's earlier disappearance was more likely to be related to a sighting of Jörgensen or Rebecca than wanting to nip back to Clapton solely for the purpose of killing Patterson.

Kyle returned to the lounge. Even for an experienced police officer Patterson's corpse was an unsettling sight, so Bates' reaction was entirely understandable.

Kyle moved around the room, carefully examining the area immediately around the body, the carpet, mantelpiece, all surfaces. Nothing seemed out of place. No foreign objects. His desk was just as he had left it, except for the obvious absence of the letter opener, an heirloom passed down from his grandparents. Somehow, Kyle couldn't see himself using it for its intended purpose in future.

The jangle of the telephone startled him. He crossed the

lounge in three strides, picked up the receiver. 'Yes?'

'Sorry for the vanishing act,' Munday's voice said. 'Had to pop off to arrange a little help. Did you get the box, or did they?'

'You spotted Jörgensen?'

'I spotted both of them.'

'Rebecca was with him?'

'Relax, she looked fine. Now, the box. Did you get there first, or did they?'

'They did.'

There was a brief silence. 'Not to worry,' Munday said. 'We'll get it back.'

'We?'

'I know where Jörgensen's headed, but this time he'll have a few friends along for the ride. He knows I'm not far behind. I'm assuming you still have young Rebecca's interests at heart?'

Kyle sighed. 'Where and when?'

'The Tower Arms car park, South Weald. Eight tonight. Got that?'

'Sure.'

The line went dead just as Bates appeared in the hall. 'Who was that?'

'A friend,' Kyle said. 'Cavalry on their way?'

'Yes. Ten minutes. DI Forsyth is taking the lead. Know him?'

'Yes.'

Bates compressed her lips and this time Kyle caught a surreptitious glance into the lounge where Patterson sat silently staring at the wall. 'No disrespect to the dead,' she said, 'but he couldn't fail to be an improvement.'

Chapter Nineteen

Kyle pulled in to the Tower Arms car park. The church clock read five fifty-five.

He locked the Mini, walked across the tarmac towards Munday, who was leaning nonchalantly on the porch timber waiting for the pub to open. 'You're early.'

Kyle nodded a greeting. 'So are you.' He dangled the keys enquiringly.

Munday shook his head. 'Keep them for now. Anything to report?'

'Your buddy, Patterson – he won't be troubling you anymore.' Kyle pocketed the keys.

Munday raised an eyebrow. 'Never my buddy, but that's not a bad mood-enhancer for starters.'

'You're not curious?'

'Reckon you're going to tell me anyway. We've a few hours to kill before the Swede turns up.'

'How can you be sure?'

Munday yawned; for a prisoner on the run he was almost preternaturally relaxed. 'He'll want to search under cover of darkness. Too many folk about at present. It's been a fine day, sun shining, spring is sprung and all that. I've had a nice walk on the Weald.'

As if in confirmation of Munday's summary a group of booted walkers strolled past the church on the other side of the lane, accompanied by two Labradors with pink tongues lolling.

Munday grinned. 'Might as well enjoy a pint while we wait. It's been a while.'

Kyle shrugged. 'If you're buying.'

A moment later the sound of rattling bolts announced that the pub was opening.

'After you.' Munday stood aside and Kyle ducked his head under the lintel and went in.

The interior of the pub smelled of old ale and woodsmoke. Kyle and Munday were joined in the bar by two council workers in overalls and another set of Weald-walkers led by a leash-straining Cocker Spaniel. Munday ordered two pints and they retired to the snug, a cosy wood-panelled room with a wide open hearth, presided over by a framed print of Landseer's *Stag at Bay*.

'Cheers.' Munday raised his glass. 'Can't tell you how much I'm going to enjoy this.'

Kyle inclined his head and took a sip. Munday seemed hearty enough but his complexion told a different story; the mildly jaundiced skin was taut over his cheekbones and his eyes were rheumy and bloodshot. The lifer's spirit might still be burning brightly, but the years of solitary had clearly taken their toll.

The ale was good, nutty and malty, the temperature spot on. Kyle replaced his glass on the table. 'You don't seem bothered that someone might clock you.'

Munday winked. 'Among friends, here. Not a problem.'

'You know it well?'

Munday nodded, placed his beer mug carefully on the mat. 'Used to drink here years ago. Got chatting with the locals.' Munday leaned in close. 'And, more importantly, with the boss. Lovely old dear, she was – Lily was her name. Ruled the place with a rod of iron.'

Munday paused for a moment's reflection, then went on. 'She told me a lot about this place. I'd heard rumours, y'see. Stories about the old house – a grand house in its day, by all accounts. Built in eighteen sixty-five or thereabouts. Anyway, it fell into disrepair eventually, and bomb damage from the war finished the job. They pulled the rest of it down along with a Belvedere that stood just to the east of the old place, overlooking the Weald.'

Munday paused again to sip his ale. Kyle waited for him to continue.

'So the rumour was that a secret room had been built under the Belvedere, along with a network of tunnels connecting the house, stable block – and maybe other locations. Lily's old man told her all about it when she was ten years old. He showed her a key – a key to a room accessible from somewhere near the Belvedere that would give access to the tunnels. Lily never wanted to explore it – superstitious, see?' Munday smiled at the memory. 'Some rumour about bad luck, maybe a ghost or two, I forget now. But, as you can well imagine I was thinking to myself; Ken old son, in your line of work, this place might come in very handy one day.'

Kyle nodded. 'I'll bet.'

'Long story short,' Munday went on, 'I persuaded Lily to let me conduct a little investigation. And lo and behold.' Munday spread his hands. 'Bingo.'

'You found the way in.'

Munday grinned. 'So, what do you think I did? I struck a

deal. Told her I'd cover the cost of re-roofing the pub in exchange for the key and a blind eye. Lily died a year later – the only other person who knew of the tunnels' existence.'

'The box,' Kyle said. 'In the *Crooked House*; that was the key.'

'Sharp as a tack, you are.'

'Odd place to hide it – in a public place.'

'Makes sense, if you think about it. Easy access. My nephew, Steve, suggested it. Good lad, Steve – he's a carpenter by trade. His dad died in a road accident so he's my son *manqué*, in many ways. Handy boxer, too.'

Kyle let that pass. The last he'd seen of Steve was at the bottom of the narrow exit stairwell of *The Crooked House*.

'You said Lily was the only other person who knew about the tunnels?' Kyle frowned. 'Sounds like you might have slipped up.'

'Yep. I told the Swede. Big mistake.' Munday drained his pint. 'But we'll sort him out.' Munday banged his mug down with a flourish. 'With your kind cooperation, Mr Kyle.'

Chapter Twenty

Kyle leaned in close and whispered. 'If someone had told me a week ago I'd be drinking with Kenneth Munday I'd have called that someone a lunatic. To be clear, this is a cooperation of convenience. I don't like being threatened and, if and when I get the chance, I'm putting you back where you belong.'

'Are you now, Mr Kyle? And that would be a citizen's arrest, would it?'

'I don't give a damn what kind of arrest it'll be, as long as I can put you behind bars. You're not safe to be out.'

Munday considered this as he took another sip of ale. He smacked his lips, put his glass down, this time lining it up with the ring of liquid the glass had left on the polished wood. 'I'm definitely not safe, but only for certain people.'

'You killed two inmates in your cell.' Kyle spoke in a low voice. 'That makes you unsafe in my book.'

'Oh, get off your bloody high horse, Kyle. You don't know what those men did. I'll spare you the details, but trust me, their crimes merited a far more severe punishment than twenty-five years of boredom.'

'So what does that make you, then? Some kind of self-appointed vigilante?'

'They got what they deserved. No more, no less. And besides, they were annoying me.' Munday ran his finger around the rim of his pint glass.

Kyle bristled, but something about Munday's bald assessment caused him to hesitate before forming a reply.

Munday was looking at him curiously. 'See? You get it, don't you? Oh sure, it runs right against your ex-copper grain, I can see that. But my way is cleaner, simpler. There are scum in this world, Mr Kyle, and they need to be got rid of.'

'And that's how you operate your business.'

Munday leaned back in his seat. 'Ah, no, different ball game, the business. No violence unless absolutely necessary – and it usually isn't, not with the fat cats I target. Tap 'em with your little finger and they crumble. If you'd care to check your records, ex-DC Kyle – and I'm sure you still have your sources – you'll find that my lads only go in after thorough research, and only take from those that can afford it.'

'So now you're a latter-day Robin Hood?'

Munday leaned forward. 'I don't mind admitting I've feathered my nest in a way that doesn't accord with the law of the land. But – and this is important – I've never taken from anyone that couldn't afford the loss. And those types – well, I'm sure I don't need to tell you that they're the sort who've, as regards the law, built their financial empires on shaky foundations – so maybe the Robin Hood comparison is more accurate than you'd imagine.'

'I suppose you donate to charity too?'

Munday smiled. 'I've done that in the past. And thanks for the reminder; I'll need to put that right when this business is over.'

Kyle picked up his glass, looked Munday in the eye. 'As

soon as I know Rebecca is safe, you'd better watch your step.'

'She'll be safe, don't worry about that.'

There was something in Munday's tone that made Kyle stop with his glass half way to his lips, but the other man had already got to his feet and was heading towards the bar.

'Not a good idea,' Kyle called after him. 'Work to do.'

Munday returned with a packet of cigarettes. 'I'm not stupid.' He waved the packet. 'Nicotine sharpens the mind.'

They left the pub via the back entrance just before eight, after Kyle had persuaded the barmaid, much to Munday's amusement, to rustle up a pot of tea. 'You have your nicotine,' Kyle said. 'I'll stick with Rosie Lee, if it's all the same to you.'

'Coffee'll keep you alert better than tea,' Munday pointed out.

'Different effect,' Kyle countered. 'Tea has a lot less caffeine but still increases alertness. It also contains a unique type of amino acid called L-theanine which increases the formation of alpha waves associated with alert relaxation. You get a milder buzz, it's gentler on the brain, and right now, that's exactly what I need. I can be alert, but relaxed. Got a problem with that?'

'No. And pardon me, Dr Kyle, for my ignorance.'

'Put it this way: tea is your granny gently encouraging you to do something. Coffee is your Sergeant-Major kicking you in the nuts.'

'Succinct.' Munday shut the door behind him. 'I'll bear it in mind.' He inspected the car park and surrounding area and, apparently satisfied, gave the signal to cross the road to the churchyard. He turned as he reached the entrance porch. 'Good vantage point from the bell tower.'

'If you say so.' Kyle glanced over his shoulder as they went in.

The smell of musty stone assailed Kyle's nostrils as they climbed the staircase to the bell tower, the slats creaking under Kyle's weight.

'I know the vicar,' Munday said. 'He won't have a problem with us being here.'

'You seem to know all the right people.' Kyle ducked his head under a beam.

'That's how I operate, Mr Kyle. It's always about who you know, not about what you do. Unless you know people, you never get anything done. Here we are – our lookout post.' Munday opened a small arched door and Kyle followed him into the tower chamber. 'I want to see how many supporters our Swedish friend has managed to rustle up.' Munday selected a cigarette and lit it.

'You seem sure Jörgensen'll show up.'

Munday blew smoke. 'He's got the key – he doesn't know where the door is, but he'll search till he finds it, that's for sure.'

'Think he'll bring Rebecca?'

'She knows too much. He'll keep her close.'

'That's what worries me.'

'She's smart, Kyle. She's already proved that. She got there first, right? Took some kids into the *Crooked House* with her, so's not to arouse suspicion. You,' Munday laughed disdainfully, 'went in on your own. You might as well have had a sign around your neck, saying: "Warning: Copper snooping around".'

'Point taken.'

'*And* she got past Steve. But you—'

'You could have warned me.' Kyle scowled.

'Wanted to see how you squared up.' Munday had a gleam in his eye. 'Steve won't hold it against you. Now, tell me about Patterson.' Munday directed smoke to one side, eyes firmly fixed on the Tower Arms car park.

Kyle shrugged. 'Someone killed him. In my flat. Fortunately I was away at the time. My ticket to the amusement park proved it.'

'No one asked you why you happened to be in Southend?'

'Sea air, good for convalescence. DI Forsyth had nothing else on me; he had to let me go.'

Munday nodded approvingly. 'So Patterson's gone. Nothing to do with me, by the way, in case you were wondering.'

'I was, as it happens.'

'Theories?'

'If not you, then Jörgensen, obviously.'

'Think he came after you?'

Kyle made a maybe-maybe-not gesture. 'I'm a loose end, I guess. Maybe he wasn't sure how much Rebecca had told me about your get-out-of-gaol plans. So, just to be on the safe side, perhaps he wanted me out of the way. If at first you don't succeed...'

'These Nordic types,' Munday said. 'They do love a bit of melodrama. Shame about the ballroom; I had a soft spot for that place.'

'Best take your wet suit if you're planning to revisit,' Kyle said. 'The orchestra'll need a diving bell for future renditions of *The Last Waltz*.'

'Engelbert. I like that song.' Munday whistled a few bars. 'Rebecca got me a radio, you know. I hadn't heard music for years.'

'She's a generous soul – she looks for the best in people. She knows how to draw that out.'

'She certainly does.'

But Kyle wasn't going to discuss Bec, not with Munday. He reached for a bell rope and waggled it experimentally. 'You and Jörgensen. I'm guessing you became … partners … during your trial?'

'Correct. Having lost in court, I said I'd still be happy to split my various earnings 25/75 if he could arrange for my exit. Took him bloody long enough.'

'So when Rebecca came along he had the perfect Trojan Horse.' Events were beginning to make sense, but Kyle frowned; something still didn't feel right, as though he were missing some significant piece of a puzzle.

'I'm not sure Rebecca would take kindly to that analogy.'

'You know *nothing* about Rebecca.' Kyle felt his hackles rise.

'On the contrary. I know a great deal.'

'Well, you'd better–'

'Wait.' Munday raised a warning hand. 'See? The blue van?'

Kyle peered through a gap in the stonework. Four men were disembarking from the back of the van that had just pulled up in the pub car park, and they didn't look like drinkers.

They looked like trouble.

Chapter Twenty-One

Kyle recognised Jörgensen's angular figure as the Swede climbed out of the driver's seat of the van. The last person to exit the vehicle caused his throat to tighten and his heart to beat a little faster; Rebecca looked unharmed, but it was clear from her body language that she was far from comfortable with her situation.

They watched as Jörgensen issued instructions. There were questions, hand gestures, some head-shaking, but the group eventually set off down the lane towards the Weald, Rebecca in front, Jörgensen immediately behind and the four heavies bringing up the rear.

'Illegals, probably,' Munday scratched his cheek. 'NFAs, no IDs, no passports. Looks like my old team's been disbanded.'

'No traceability.' Kyle nodded. 'Hence easily disposable.'

'Just as well, don't you think?' Munday waited until Jörgensen's party had disappeared from view before turning to Kyle. 'Ready?'

'Always.'

They descended from the bell tower, Kyle still half-expecting to be buttonholed and cross-examined by the vicar, or waylaid by some security-conscious verger, but they exited the church without incident and made their way through the churchyard, passing unseen beneath the lychgate and into the lane.

Dusk was falling as Kyle followed Munday along a narrow trackway that ran parallel with and slightly above the lane. As he ducked to avoid the roof of overhanging branches he realised that his headache had gone. For the first time since his injury, the constant pressure had vanished. No time now to worry about what that might mean – Munday had arrived at a wooden stile and his arm was raised to signal a temporary halt.

'So where now?' Kyle surveyed the Weald. Woodland to the left, grassy slopes ahead and to the right all the way down to the largest of the area's lakes. To the north-east the skeletal remains of a lightning-blasted oak tree stood sentinel-like against the lighter backdrop of the lake.

'I know what they're thinking,' Munday sneered. 'Same as everyone else – that the entrance is somewhere at the *base* of the twin staircases, where the belvedere – or the folly, as it was commonly known – used to be.'

'It's not?'

Munday said nothing. Which meant either that the logical inference of his last statement was crystal clear and needed no explanation, or that he just wanted Kyle to believe it to be true. Kyle was keeping an open mind. Munday was his ally only in the current moment; that would change as soon as Kyle saw an opportunity to free Rebecca. Munday knew this, of course, and knew that Kyle knew he knew. So Kyle didn't press for an answer.

'There's a way in, and a way out,' Munday said. 'But they won't find either easily. And that, my tall friend, gives us a distinct advantage. So, before we get stuck in, let's think about deployment of resources.'

Kyle leaned on the rough wood of the stile. 'OK. Sven will

be keeping Rebecca close. So, of the four guys he has with him, I'd say two to search, two to keep guard.'

'And I'd agree. The folly sits in a small clearing. We get to it over yonder.' Munday pointed to a gap in the wooded area to their left. 'The path rises fairly steeply, but there's good cover on either side.'

'I'll go left.'

'Good.' Munday's hand reached into his jacket, and came out holding the pistol. 'Sorry. Just one between us, I'm afraid. But then, you coppers aren't used to handling firearms, are you?'

'Ex-coppers.'

Munday gave a short laugh. 'You'll be useful enough in a fight. Just don't forget I have this.' He held the pistol in front of Kyle. 'Be a good lad. No funny stuff while I'm not looking.'

'Perish the thought.'

Munday nodded, pocketed the handgun. 'Shall we?'

Munday vaulted the stile and Kyle followed suit. They moved quickly across the open ground to the gap Munday had indicated. Kyle went left, keeping just inside the tree line; a glance to his right confirmed that Munday was mirroring his movements on the opposite side, stealthily moving in a half-crouch from tree to tree, stopping to listen, giving his night vision time to kick in before moving on.

It wasn't long before Kyle saw torchlight flickering somewhere up ahead. Normally he would have given himself plenty of time to work through how best to approach what was essentially an unknown and highly volatile situation. Tonight, though, he felt different – but that was no surprise. *Everything* was different now. Sure, he might get himself killed, but so what? He just wanted to get on with it – he'd deal with Munday as and when the opportunity presented itself.

He moved from tree to tree until he was close to the stone steps that were all that remained of the folly and belvedere. There was someone half way up the flight on the left-hand side, a dark silhouette against a grey-black sky. 'Hands up.' A guttural voice spoke behind him. The accent was a mixture of Eastern European and Hollywood gangster which, Kyle supposed, was logical, given that American movies were probably where the owner of the voice had likely picked up most of his English vocabulary.

He obliged, raising his arms as he slowly turned to face his would-be captor. Kyle recognised him as the last of Sven's helpers to get out of the van; he was bullet-headed, stocky and gap-toothed, a feature clearly displayed as his mouth twisted into a wide, anticipatory smile. 'That's good. I want to see your face, how it looks, when I make all the holes in your chest.'

Kyle was pleased the guy had asked him to lift his arms, because that meant his hands were near the overhanging branch. The tree was an oak, so Kyle wasn't worried that the bough might not bear his weight. Before his European friend could speak again he reached for the branch and swung his legs up in one easy movement, at once making himself a smaller target and at the same time using his legs to encircle bullet-head's neck. Kyle had reasoned that provided he was quick, Sven's henchman would be more concerned about choking to death than worrying about what his pistol hand was doing.

It turned out Kyle was right. The guy instinctively

dropped the gun, raising both hands to his neck to try to free himself from the brutal grip of Kyle's quadriceps, twin-muscles honed by a lifetime of rugby training. He tried to yell, but Kyle's grip was relentless. It was over in under a minute.

Kyle unwrapped his legs and dropped lightly to the ground as his adversary crumpled and hit the earth like a carelessly dropped sack of potatoes. He felt for a pulse. Unconscious, but still alive. Nicely judged.

Kyle started to clean his mossy hands on his trousers, but then thought better of it and instead smeared the green substance on his cheeks, forehead, nose. All the better if they couldn't see him coming. He took a breath.

One down, four to go.

Five, if you included Munday.

Chapter Twenty-Two

The folly steps led to nowhere – just a grassy bank, from the top of which it was possible to look down into the clearing below. The centre section of the bank had been bricked up, giving it the appearance of a blocked tunnel entrance. Did Munday's tunnels lie behind this earthwork? Or beneath it?

Kyle surveyed the clearing from his vantage point at the foot of the steps. Torchlight flickered briefly somewhere on the far side of the folly and Jörgensen's voice, amplified by the shape of the stonework echoed drily across the grass, berating one of the heavies, or perhaps encouraging them to search harder. Then a woman's voice, raised in anger, followed by the sound of a palm on flesh, the voice abruptly cut off. Kyle's fists bunched at his sides.

A shadow moved in front of the brickwork, a torch beam played momentarily on the façia and abruptly clicked off. Searcher number one, moving methodically along the folly's base, looking for a gap in the render or some lever that would reveal an entrance. Was he alone? Kyle moved in a half-crouch to the near end of the steps, and waited for the guy to come to him.

The torch flickered again, then cut off. Kyle flattened himself against the stonework. A match flared in the darkness and the harsh smell of cigarette smoke drifted across to where Kyle was waiting. A shout broke the silence.

'Ay? Anything yet?'

The voice came from above, somewhere on the top of the mound. Kyle was still glued to the staircase.

The nearest man called back. 'Nah. Nothing. Is waste of time.'

'Keep looking. That's what he pays us for, OK?'

'Sure.'

Soft footsteps receded above.

The smoker drew closer and closer to where Kyle was standing, muttering to himself. Kyle caught a word he thought might have been *Swede*, or *Sweden*. He calculated it would be ten to fifteen seconds before the smoker was close enough to grab, but in that he was mistaken; the guy's patience was almost at an end. Without warning, he abandoned his inch-by-inch examination and shone the torch along the length of the monument base.

The light played at Kyle's feet, halted, and then jerked up towards his face, but by then Kyle had already launched himself in a full-length rugby tackle. He smashed into the guy just below his midriff and brought him crashing to earth before he could make a sound. Kyle's weight drove the the air from the other man's lungs, and while he was preoccupied with trying to breath Kyle's fist connected with the side of his head, his eyes rolled up in their sockets and his body went limp.

Kyle dragged him into the trees, undid his belt and trussed his hands behind his back. He extracted cigarettes and a box of Swan Vestas from his pocket, and as an afterthought he also removed the unconscious man's shoes and chucked them into a thick growth of bramble. Hard to fight without footwear.

124

He moved back to the edge of the clearing and checked to see if the disturbance had alerted Jörgensen's remaining hard men, or even the Swede himself, but the woods were still and silent. Where was Munday? Had he accounted for Jörgensen's two other buddies, or had they found him first? Kyle parked that thought. Rebecca was his priority, and she was most likely still with Jörgensen.

He moved silently towards the folly and stopped at the foot of the steps. What had Munday said?

I know what they're thinking ... same as everyone else – that the entrance is somewhere at the base of the twin staircases...

Kyle climbed the first two steps. If there was no entrance behind the brick façade, then there might be one higher up. Logic suggested it wouldn't be too far up, otherwise whoever had constructed the tunnels would also have needed to create a corresponding route to return to ground level.

Kyle considered an eighteenth century builder's mindset. Then, as now, labour – especially clandestine labour – would have been expensive, so short cuts would probably have been taken wherever possible. So, an entrance at ground level, or very near ground level, made sense. Kyle reached the sixth step, around nine feet from the ground. The next riser, he noticed, was a little larger than the preceding ones. He stamped his foot experimentally on the sixth step, and then tried the next; sure enough, it produced a subtly different noise, less solid, perhaps indicative of an open space below.

His probing fingers explored the contours and recessed handholds cut into each side of the stone slab. He was impressed; they were almost undetectable from above. He got a good grip on each side and pulled. It came up surprisingly easily.

Kyle propped it against the bank to his left and lifted the iron ring in the centre of the trapdoor he'd uncovered. That, too opened easily. Those Georgian architects knew what they were about. Kyle peered into the interior.

Ten rungs led down into a dark shaft, at the bottom of which he could make out an earthen floor that looked solid enough to bear his weight. Now it was time to share his discovery. He lit a cigarette, took three deep pulls and placed it on the step above the opening. Then he cupped his hands around his mouth and yelled an invitation.

'Hey! I have it.'

He lowered himself into the shaft, taking the steps one at a time until his feet touched the bottom. He lit a match and looked around. He was in a small room with two possible exits, not counting the one he had entered by. He went to the nearest opening, ducked his head to avoid the crossbeam and moved quickly along the narrow corridor. A few seconds later he came to a blockage. There was no way through; the tunnel had either been collapsed deliberately or had fallen in over time.

Dead end.

He retraced his steps to the entrance, paused briefly before passing beneath the tunnel until he was satisfied that Jörgensen's minders had yet to arrive, then crossed quickly to the second opening. This looked more promising. It led off to the right, towards the church, and was a wider, taller construction. Whereas the first tunnel had felt airless and disused, this route was wide open and the airflow was good. Before he had time to explore further he heard voices above, a scrabbling of feet. A torch beam shone into the chamber from the access port, formed a ragged pool of light that lit the small room in a diffused, orange glow.

Kyle waited in the shadow of the second tunnel until he had counted the measured descents of two pairs of feet, then made his way along the passage until he came to the first bend. He knew they'd do the obvious thing; they'd take an opening each. One would explore the dead end tunnel, the other would come his way. That suited Kyle. It meant he could deal with them one at a time.

Less than a minute later he heard the sound of cautious footsteps, a probing torch beam announcing the arrival of number one.

'Yuri? *Yuri?*'

Kyle pressed his back against the tunnel's damp wall. The man called out again, a series of frustrated phrases in his own language that weren't hard to interpret.

Where the hell are you, Yuri?

Kyle guessed that Yuri would be waking up with a severe headache in around an hour or so. But that was his problem. The footsteps drew closer. Just before the man reached the bend Kyle stepped from the shadows, and before the other had time to react he delivered a fast right uppercut to the chin. Yuri's buddy reeled back against the wall with a grunt, and the torch jolted in his hand, the beam tracking briefly across Kyle's face before it dropped to the floor. A millisecond before the tunnel was plunged into darkness Kyle caught sight of the revolver in the guy's other hand.

Momentarily blinded, Kyle moved forward, arms raised, towards the spot where the man had fallen. His adversary was down but not out; using the tunnel wall as a springboard, he propelled himself forward and hit Kyle dead centre. They tumbled to the floor, tangled together, but Kyle knew the other guy wouldn't be keen to engage in a bout of prolonged physical combat, not now that he'd had the chance to clock Kyle's build. No, he would be looking for the revolver he'd dropped.

But to do that, he had to release Kyle and make a grab for it. The man's head was close to Kyle's, his breath sour in his face. Kyle waited for him to let go and commit himself to lunge either right or left; it was a gamble and it could go either way, but then every moment of Kyle's current existence was a gamble of sorts. Like a dream-sequence from a movie, everything seemed to slow down; Kyle felt a sensation of light-headedness, but also an overwhelming sense of calm. If he died, he died. Hell, he had to die sometime; in an hour, or tomorrow, or any time. So what?

The guy rolled off him and went left; Kyle went right. His hands swept the floor, connected immediately with a cold, metallic grip. His finger curled round the trigger.

A sudden, breathless silence filled the tunnel; the other man knew he had just lost. Kyle sprang to his feet, took careful aim at the dark outline crouched in front of him, and brought the butt of the revolver down on his head. The man rolled over and lay still.

Three down, one to go.

Two, if you counted Jörgensen.

Chapter Twenty-Three

'Hey? You there? Is dead end here. No damn good.'

The second man's confident footsteps gave Kyle a good indication that he wasn't expecting trouble. This time Kyle waited a little longer before announcing his presence because he'd found a better place to wait; twenty yards further on, where the tunnel made an almost ninety-degree turn to the right. He'd dragged the first man along with him, dumping the unconscious form behind an ancient trestle table propped against the nearside wall.

Kyle waited until his mate had moved a foot or so past him before stepping out and wrapping his arm around the thick-set neck.

'Drop it.'

The man froze, did as he was told, and his weapon fell to the floor. Keeping one arm firmly locked around the other man's throat, Kyle hissed a second instruction. 'Bend, nice and slow.'

They bent together and Kyle retrieved the automatic, slipped it into his pocket. He released his hold, just a little. 'Now, I'm asking nicely. Where is Jörgensen?'

The man responded in a stream of his mother tongue. Kyle tutted. 'I already know you speak English, albeit pidgin, so let's try again. Where is Jörgensen?'

More Eastern European invective.

Kyle tightened his grip again, tutted. 'I hate swearing. It's ugly. But coming from you, it kind of fits. Speak nicely or not at all, got it?'

The man gurgled. He understood well enough.

'I'll find him easily enough without you, but I'm not wasting the rest of my evening playing night games. I've better things to do, understand?'

Kyle eased the pressure a fraction and number four took a shuddering breath.

'There you go. Much nicer when you can breathe, isn't it?'

'The church. He said he goes to the church.'

'He said that? When?'

'I don't know, ten minutes, or something.'

'Or something.'

'Yes. He said that. Is the truth.'

'Good. The church it is, then.'

Kyle twisted the man through a hundred and eighty degrees and hit him hard. He sank silently to the floor.

Kyle spend a few minutes trussing the two men together and stuffing a handkerchief in each mouth. When he was satisfied they were securely tied, he took the torch and carried on along the tunnel. By his reckoning it was heading in precisely the right direction.

After a couple of minutes the tunnel began to narrow and Kyle noticed that there was now a definite incline, another indicator that the tunnel was a direct route to the church. However, the torch he'd borrowed must have sustained damage because it soon began to flicker and then died altogether.

Kyle paused to strike a match. The sudden flare highlighted a line of graffiti on the wall ahead:

Abandon hope all ye who enter here

Kyle pressed on regardless. Hope was an uncertain premise; Kyle's preference was for direct action. He wondered if the line had been penned by some eighteenth century subaltern, or maybe just a builder with a warped sense of humour.

The match burned out and he lit another – noticing as he did so the stump of an old candle lying on the lid of a mildewed wooden chest. Kyle lit the candle and then, out of curiosity, opened the chest. It was empty except for a lining of newspaper. The date of the yellowed *Daily Mail* was August 1954.

Kyle closed the lid and moved on. Wherever Munday had stashed his money it certainly wasn't going to be found in a random, unlocked box.

The candle cast unnerving shadows on the tunnel walls as the gradient sloped up and up. Surely he must be nearly there? The tunnel bent to the right again and following it, Kyle was suddenly confronted by a dead end; the only way out was a metal ladder bolted to the brickwork. He raised the candle above his head. The ladder led to a bolted hatch some fifteen feet above.

He tested the ladder's stability, put his foot on the first rung. It seemed good and solid. He climbed a couple more rungs and they held steady. At the top, he let wax from the candle drip onto the top rung and fixed the candle in place while he got to work on the bolts. One drew relatively easily after a few hard tugs. The other, following the general rule of things that needed to be unfastened, didn't want to move at all.

He could see that the door hadn't been accessed for a very long time; a wide lattice of spider's web hung beneath the wood of the hatch like a miniature safety net. The candle was burning low, and Kyle didn't much fancy mucking around in the dark, especially when he had no idea what might be waiting for him once he'd got the hatch open.

He hefted the automatic, banged the butt against the recalcitrant bolt. It gave a little, so he hit it again. This time it slid open with a small shower of rust flakes. He pocketed the gun, pushed experimentally at the trapdoor with both hands; it gave a creak and opened a fraction, letting in a puff of stale air. Kyle cautiously stuck his head through, felt for the candle and held it aloft.

'Perfect,' Jörgensen's voice said. 'Do *not* move. I am an excellent shot.'

Kyle ducked down and let the trapdoor fall with a crash. The report of Jörgensen's pistol followed an instant later.

Not excellent enough…

Kyle swung himself to the left of the shaft, clung to the side of the ladder. Four more shots punctured the wood and whistled past his head before the trapdoor was wrenched open and Jörgensen's face appeared in the gap.

'Don't be a bloody idiot, Kyle.'

This time, Kyle complied. He was a sitting duck; even if he went for the automatic, Jörgensen would shoot him like a rat in a trap before he could even aim his own firearm.

'I'd raise my hands, but I'm using them.'

Jörgensen gave a mirthless laugh. 'Just keep them where I can see them, and climb up *very* slowly. I have found the ideal resting place for you.'

Chapter Twenty-Four

Kyle heaved himself through the small aperture. It was only just wide enough for his shoulders; either eighteenth-century builders were very slight in stature, or they just hadn't considered someone of Kyle's build.

Jörgensen played his torch at Kyle's feet. 'Want to know what I found?'

'Munday's treasure box? Good for you.'

Kyle looked around him. They were in the church crypt; rows of wall-mounted ledges groaned under the weight of two hundred years' worth of dead people.

'Albert Cheeseman, went to sleep January 12th 1899,' Jörgensen quoted. 'May his soul rest in peace.'

'Ah. Don't tell me. Mr Cheeseman had to make way for something of greater value.'

Jörgensen guffawed. 'Ten thousand pounds in ten pound notes, to be exact.'

'Here? In the crypt?' Kyle was thinking about the key.

'Almost. Come this way, if you please, DC Kyle.'

'*Ex*-DC Kyle.'

'Walk in front of me, if you wouldn't mind. Thank you.'

'Where's Rebecca?'

'You'll see.'

They made their way along the earthen floor of the crypt. Many of the coffins had rotted, their crumbling lids exposing the contents; grinning skulls animated by Jörgensen's dancing torchlight. Kyle paid them scant attention; he was thinking hard. Jörgensen had passed on the opportunity to kill him outright. Sure, the Swede was probably planning on something terminal – but only after he'd shown Kyle the money. That fitted with Kyle's character assessment; Jörgensen's ego would be his downfall. Kyle followed his usual rule of thumb: keep your opponent talking…

'You're on your own, Jörgensen. Your hired buddies are otherwise engaged.'

Jörgensen stuck the pistol into the small of Kyle's back. 'Do I care? I found what I came for; and you are no longer a problem. Stop here. Go up.'

They had reached a set of stone steps that presumably led up into the body of the church. Kyle did as he was told; the steps terminated at a heavy iron door, into which an inspection grille had been cut. Kyle stood in front of the door and waited.

'Go on. Open it.'

Kyle slid the grille open and looked into a tiny room, almost a cell. Rebecca was sitting on the floor, gagged and bound. Her eyes widened as she saw Kyle peering in. There was a coffin against the opposite wall from where Rebecca was sitting, the unfortunate Mr Cheeseman's, presumably. The lid was open and Kyle could see bundles of notes inside.

'If you would be kind enough to hold the torch. Point it towards the lock.'

The pistol dug into Kyle's back as Jörgensen gave him the torch.

Jörgensen inserted Munday's key and turned it. 'You know what this place is?

'I'm guessing you're about to tell me.'

'An anchoress' cell. See, up there? That was a window, so she could look into the church. It was sealed long ago, and no one comes in here – but now, there is a new anchoress. And you will join her in her ascetic vigil.'

'I'm charmed.'

Jörgensen was enjoying himself. 'But your vigil will be short-lived. In the days of the anchoress, the faithful congregation would see to her earthly needs. But how long will you both survive without water? Without food? The floor above – it is thick, solid. No one will hear you. No one will know you are here. Maybe you will be discovered by some future generation. An archaeological marvel, hm? Perhaps they will place you in a museum.'

'My mother always wanted me to make my mark.'

'The water failed to claim you; now the earth will swallow you.'

Kyle thought he'd heard something, a surreptitious sound from the crypt. Rats? Or maybe–'

'Sit down.'

The pistol was still pointing directly at him; Jörgensen couldn't miss. He stood next to Rebecca. Her eyes were twin ovals of fear.

'Torch, please, Mr Kyle.'

Kyle made as if to hand it over. 'You finally lost the *DC*. Well remembered.'

As Jörgensen reached for the torch Kyle heard the noise again, the soft tread of plimsolled feet. Jörgensen glanced towards the cell door. Kyle shone the torch directly in Jörgensen's face, then shut the beam off. The room was plunged into darkness.

Jörgensen fired the pistol. The cell lit up momentarily in the muzzle flash, and in that brief millisecond Kyle saw Munday lying full-length on the top step, both arms extended in front of him. Two further shots rang out. Jörgensen screamed.

Kyle flicked the torch button.

Jörgensen lay on his back clutching his legs; blood was seeping from gunshot wounds in both limbs, spreading in an irregular pool around him.

Munday picked himself up, dusted himself down. 'Floor's filthy. I thought cleanliness was next to godliness.'

The room stank of cordite. Jörgensen was panting through clenched teeth. 'Call a doctor. I'm bleeding to death.'

Munday affected a brief inspection. 'Give me some credit. I missed both arteries. You'll live.'

Kyle turned his attention to Rebecca, untied her gag. 'Are you OK? Did he–?'

'I'm *fine*, Cam. Just get these off me.'

Kyle undid Rebecca's bonds and she stood up, rubbed her legs and wrists. She went to the prone Jörgensen, kicked him hard in the groin. 'You *bastard*.'

Jörgensen howled, curled himself into a ball.

Kyle moved to restrain her but Munday got there first. To Kyle's astonishment, they fell into each others arms. 'I thought I'd lost you,' Munday was whispering. 'I thought he'd killed you.'

'I'm fine, I'm OK, really.' Rebecca tightened her arms around Munday. 'I *knew* you'd come. I knew it.'

Kyle's mouth opened and closed as he looked at them in disbelief. His gaze tracked from the entwined couple, to the coffin of bank notes, to Jörgensen and then back again.

What…?

He leaned on the cell door frame, sparks of light dancing before his eyes. Nausea swept through him and his vision began to blur. He managed to sit on the step, hold his head in his hands.

Somewhere high above, the church clock struck the hour, a long, resonant clanging that reverberated through the stone walls. For Kyle, it signalled the end of hope.

Chapter Twenty-Five

'DC Bates. Who's calling?'

'Kyle here,' Kyle said. 'I have a criminal in custody. Well, several, actually.'

'Kyle? Where *are* you? Have you *any* idea of the time?'

'Sorry, couldn't wait.'

'This had *better* be good – anyhow, my new guv wants to spea—'

'Forsyth can join the party later. I think you should see this for yourself.'

A pause. 'OK. Where are you?'

Kyle gave Bates the address, signed off and left the phone box. He glanced wistfully at the Tower Arms, but last orders would have been called a long time ago. The village was settled and still, the silence broken only by the hourly tolling of the church bell.

Munday and Rebecca had long gone; only Jörgensen's blue van remained in the car park, Jörgensen himself safely incarcerated in the anchoress' cell, along with his hired hands. The four had had little fight left in them when they'd rounded them up at gunpoint and marched them along the road to join Jörgensen, just abusive words in a tongue neither Munday nor Kyle had understood.

An examination of the Swede's injuries had proved that Munday's assessment was correct; the damage was superficial, both bullets having passed through Jörgensen's flesh causing neither arterial nor skeletal damage. While Kyle – and Rebecca for that matter – would have been content to let Jörgensen bleed to death, Munday had insisted on the application of temporary tourniquets.

'Be gutted to think he might miss out on a twenty-five year stretch,' Munday had explained. 'I wouldn't sleep at night.'

Rebecca had avoided eye contact. There was a lot Kyle wanted to say to her, but he knew this was neither the time nor the place.

Kyle sat on a bench in front of the pub. The church tower was silhouetted against the night sky like a giant finger pointing to the heavens; Kyle wondered what the good Lord would make of the ungodly quintet locked in the anchoress' cell.

He reckoned Bates would take an hour or so to make the journey. As he settled down to wait, he began to turn over in his mind the events of the past couple of days, from Rebecca's unexpected visit to tonight's discovery of Munday's tunnels. It had been bad enough to think of her with Jörgensen, but this latest revelation had knocked him for six. Easy enough, though, to see how it might have happened. Rebecca, sincere, humane, empathetic, and Munday, startlingly intelligent, articulate and, Kyle begrudgingly conceded, not bad looking for his age. They'd initially been thrown together by circumstance and necessity, but as time had gone on, as they had gradually got to know one another, something else had crept in, something unexpected but compellingly irresistible; they'd fallen for one another.

As Kyle contemplated his ex's new liaison, he felt an

overpowering urge to chain-smoke the remainder of the cigarettes he'd taken from Jörgensen's buddy earlier in the evening. He managed to resist; it might give his hands something to do, but, he reasoned, it wouldn't do his returning headache much good.

He considered the prison escape. Far from being escorted from the building against her will, Rebecca had apparently been a willing accomplice. Maybe she had already decided to ditch Jörgensen, or perhaps she had even suspected that he was not what he claimed to be. Perhaps Munday himself had warned her, explained that rather than continuing in his capacity as Munday's agent, his partner-in-crime had made the decision to work independently. Kyle surmised that Munday's man in the ballroom had probably been tasked with the Swede's disposal, after which Rebecca was to have paid him off and rendezvoused with Munday with the rest of the money.

But Kyle's involvement, the fact that Rebecca had visited him, had unsettled Jörgensen. The Swede couldn't be sure how much Rebecca had told him. Kyle realised now that she had come to him because she had genuinely wanted to know if Munday could be trusted, if he could really be a reformed character and not the monster the newspapers would have the public believe. It was a small consolation to Kyle that she'd sought his advice, that there was still enough residual respect, even trust, between them that she had gone out of her way to seek his opinion.

Kyle took out a cigarette and tapped it on the packet. Jörgensen had been smart. He'd known that Kyle would come running if Rebecca was in danger. He had wanted Kyle where he could see him, so he could dispose of

Rebecca, Kyle and whoever else happened to be in the way at the time. And where better than an abandoned estate, an underwater ballroom?

Kyle broke the cigarette in half, threw the pieces away. The wind soughed in the trees and the moon slipped from behind a cloud. An owl hooted and was still. There was no discernible traffic noise, even though the Weald wasn't far from the main road; if it wasn't for the presence of Jörgensen's blue van, the scene might well have been from a century or more earlier.

The hands of the church clock moved slowly and Kyle stayed where he was, eyes half-closed, his mind wandering. Another hour passed before he snapped awake at the sound of a car engine labouring up the hill behind the pub.

He stood up and rubbed his weary limbs as a blue Ford Anglia appeared around the corner, came to a halt by the church. DC Bates got out, crossed the road with a waved greeting. She didn't look happy.

'You're aware it's the middle of the night?'

'Sorry. It's inconvenient, I know.'

'A girl needs her beauty sleep.'

'There's always tomorrow night.'

Bates yawned. 'Too far away. So, what's up?'

Kyle offered her a seat next to him on the bench. 'Long story.'

When he'd finished, Bates was silent for a moment before shooting him a suspicious look. 'This is for real, yes? You're not spinning me some yarn for God knows what reason?'

'I'm not. It's for real.'

'There are five men locked in a cell under the church, one of whom probably needs medical attention.'

'Yep.'

'And Munday? You let him drive away?'

Kyle shrugged. 'What choice did I have? He still had the gun. Besides, he's not all bad.'

'He's a convicted criminal, Kyle. He killed people.'

'He killed people who didn't deserve to live, if that's what you're referring to.'

Bates sighed, shook her head. 'I'm going to have to call this in, you know that, don't you?'

'I do, but there are one or two things I need to talk about first.'

'Namely?'

'Let's backtrack to my flat. Patterson. How's that investigation going?'

Bates looked at her hands. 'Slowly. Forsyth's coming round to the idea that it was probably some opportunist burglary. Patterson was there at the wrong time.'

'Maybe.' Kyle looked at her.

'You think otherwise?' She glanced up and the moonlight caught her hair. Not for the first time, Kyle noticed how pretty she was.

'Just tell me you were wearing gloves at the time.'

'Excuse me?'

Kyle looked her in the eye. 'You heard.'

'Gloves? I – I, yes, of course. It was a crime scene. I'm always careful, I–'

This was delicate. As gently as he could, Kyle said, 'DC Bates, was DI Patterson harassing you right from the start? Or was it more of a gradual process?'

Chapter Twenty-Six

There was a long silence, broken only by the breeze in the trees. When Bates looked up, her eyes were filmed with tears. 'It's OK,' Kyle said. 'I get it.'

'How did you know?'

'There are always signs. Body language. The way you kept your distance from him. The way he looked at you.'

'That obvious?'

'Afraid so.' Kyle found the cigarettes, offered the pack. Bates took one and Kyle lit it with the last Swan Vesta.

'Thanks.' Bates drew in smoke, exhaled.

'I probably would have done the same in your situation.'

The silence that followed was like a vacuum, a black hole. The breeze dropped and the leaves were stilled. Smoke rose from Bates' cigarette. Ash fell unheeded from its cinder tip. Eventually Bates asked, 'How did you know it was me?'

'There were clues – and forgive me if this sounds a bit glib, but I *was* a detective until fairly recently.'

'A good one, clearly.' Bates shivered and Kyle resisted the urge to put his arm around her. Now was definitely not the moment. 'So,' she said, 'what clues, exactly?'

'When I went to fetch you a drink I noticed that the level in the Metaxa bottle had gone down a little. Not much, only a very small amount, but it meant you'd already had a nip to steady your nerves after you killed him – and by the way, I'm sure you didn't intend to kill him. But you made a big thing of not recognising – and not liking, for that matter – the Metaxa when I offered it to you.'

Bates tapped ash with her forefinger. 'It was actually horrible – but you didn't have any whisky.'

'Can't stand the stuff. Anyway, the other thing was that you didn't immediately consider me a suspect, even though I could have been in the vicinity at the time – I mean, I arrived what? Five, ten minutes after it happened? Under normal circumstances you'd have started to interrogate me before I even stepped into my flat.'

Bates' composure was wobbling. 'You're right, of course. I didn't mean to kill him.' She threw her cigarette on the ground, buried her face in her hands. Now Kyle did put his arm around her.

'It's OK. No one has to know.'

She looked up and her tear-stained face was white in the moonlight. 'They'll find out, Kyle. They'll know.'

Kyle shook his head. 'Even if they did, the circumstances'd be taken into account. I bet you have witnesses among your colleagues willing to back you. Did you mention it to anyone?'

'Only to Anne – DC Keogh. She knew something was up.'

'There you go.'

'But I still killed a man.'

Kyle gripped her shoulders. 'A trusted senior officer attacked you. I'm guessing he tried it on, you pushed him away, he shoved you against my desk, you felt for something to defend yourself, and there was the letter opener. Correct?'

She nodded miserably.

'Self defence in any court of law.'

'You think?'

'Yes. But it's not going to get that far.'

'How? I don't understand.'

'You were *definitely* wearing gloves?'

'Yes.'

'Good, because Jörgensen's prints will be all over the letter opener – as well as mine, but it's my property, and I have an alibi. He doesn't.'

'Wait … how will his prints be on the letter opener?'

'He came to ask for help the morning Bec – Rebecca – went missing. He opened an envelope he'd brought with him – supposedly from Munday – giving directions to Weald Hall. He probably wrote it himself.'

Bates gave a stiff nod.

'So your story is that Jörgensen and Munday were in cahoots – which, as we now know, they originally were. Jörgensen kills Patterson on Munday's say so – Patterson was the officer who put Munday away, so there's your motive. But then they fall out. Jörgensen tries to snatch Munday's hidden assets with a little help from his illegals – you can check in Jörgensen's van for evidence they came with him – but Munday gets the better of the situation, locks them up and disappears. Meanwhile, I, concerned for Rebecca's safety, followed up on something she once said about South Weald, which I'll say I only remembered yesterday. When I got here I found Jörgensen and party locked up with a firearm and a suspicious amount of money. Naturally I called my police contact immediately. And here you are.'

'It's all Wealds with Munday, isn't it? Weald House, South Weald…' Bates tried to raise the corners of her mouth and almost succeeded.

It was a good effort. Kyle rewarded it by giving her hand a reassuring squeeze. 'Some subconscious connection, I imagine.'

Bates made no attempt to withdraw her hand. 'What about Munday?'

Kyle took a deep breath. 'I've met worse. Munday had a bad start in life. It wasn't his fault. OK, he killed a few people. But they were low-lifes – there's no doubt that that's what they were, so no loss. In fact, you could look at it that he did the world a favour. Having spent a little time with Munday I'm coming around to his way of thinking.'

'So we let him walk?'

'I don't think you'll hear much from him. I certainly don't think he'll reoffend.'

'But what if he's caught? He'll contest my – *your* – version of events.'

'He's too smart to get caught a second time; he'll keep the lowest possible profile. He won't be out and about much, you can bet on that.'

'I don't know if Forsyth will buy this, Kyle.'

'Course he will. He wants a result, doesn't he? This way, he gets to solve a murder, reimburse the Treasury with at least a percentage of Munday's illicit wealth, *and* deport four passport-less hooligans to wherever they came from. Trust me, the Chief Constable will love it.'

Bates sighed. 'All right. I don't know what to say. I don't understand why you're helping me like this.'

'I like you Bates,' Kyle said truthfully. 'And I don't like seeing people abused and misused, as you've been.'

Bates was silent, chewed her lip.

He released her hand and stood up. 'Ready to call it in?'

'As I'll ever be.' Bates tried the smile again and this time it worked. 'One thing…'

'What?'

'I've only known you a short while, but Patterson had you all wrong.'

Kyle grimaced. 'I'm not sure I know myself. Not this version, anyhow.'

'Well, I don't care what you were like before. I like the new version.'

'I'll have to get used to it, I suppose. I haven't much choice,' Kyle said. 'For however long I'm around.'

Chapter Twenty-Seven

'They'll be here anytime.' Bates rechecked her watch.

'Better check on our buddies, make sure they're behaving.' Kyle got up, stretched his legs. Even if Jörgensen was making a racket, no one would hear him. As the Swede had pointed out, the crypt was too far underground for noise to carry.

'Not without me you're not.'

They took the path to the church, found the side door through which Kyle had exited earlier and went down the stone staircase towards the crypt.

Bates said, 'Are you going to tell Forsyth about the tunnels?'

Kyle considered this. 'Let's not complicate things. They have everything they need in the cell, so I doubt whether they'll search the wider area. A cursory check, perhaps, but Forsyth will want to get them banged up as soon as possible.' They arrived at the point where the stairwell divided. 'Careful here,' he advised. 'This is a tight squeeze.'

They eased themselves onto the set of narrower steps and Kyle marvelled again at the guile of the original stonemasons who'd fashioned the entrance to the anchoress' cell so artfully that it was almost entirely invisible from the main staircase.

It was uncannily quiet as they arrived at the cell door. Kyle slid the grille open. There was no one in his line of sight except a pair of legs. Kyle recognised the shoes. Jörgensen. Where were the heavies? He glanced behind him and Bates shot him a quizzical look. Kyle closed the grille and cautiously unbarred the door. 'This isn't good,' he warned. Jörgensen was half-lying, half-sitting against the far wall. The hired hands were gone, but Jörgensen wasn't going anywhere. Kyle bent and performed a rapid examination. There was a small wound directly over his heart. A thin blade, a quick entry – an instant death. Kyle had seen such wounds before. Only one weapon fitted the bill: a stiletto.

Bates ground the cigarette beneath her heel. 'Great. Now what do I tell Forsyth?'

'Tell him the truth. I told you the cell was occupied by five men, all alive. You had no reason to disbelieve me. Since you called it in, the situation changed – you have no idea how or why – but as you were on your own, keeping a watchful eye on me was your priority. Eventually you suggested that we should reassess the situation before the posse arrived. Ergo, you can only surmise that someone went in and out quick, freed the hired guns and disposed of Jörgensen while you were being briefed by my good self.'

'But it looks *totally* incompetent.' Bates paced up and down. 'I should have gone straight in to check.'

'Come on,' Kyle said. 'No one would have expected you to tackle a situation like that on your own. I'll back you up.'

'No disrespect, but Forsyth won't be satisfied with that.'

'Let's try to figure out what actually *did* happen,' Kyle sat on the bench. 'Someone was watching us. That same someone waited for us to withdraw, went in the back way, via the tunnels, coerced the grunts, killed Jörgensen.'

'Those guys must have known who it was, or they wouldn't have gone with him.'

'Agreed.'

'And the money?'

'Gone, of course.'

'Could it have been Munday? Maybe he doubled back, and–'

'Why? He already had the lion's share of the stash. What he left behind was supposed to incriminate Jörgensen.'

Bates had stopped fretting, now she was thinking. 'And he had the chance to kill Jörgensen earlier in any case, but he didn't take it. So you say.' She glanced down at him.

'Now you don't believe me?'

'God, Kyle.' She joined him on the bench. 'I don't know *what* to believe any more.'

'Well, you'd better make up your mind. Here's Forsyth and co.' The ululation of multiple sirens split the early morning air, engines revving, changing gear as they tackled the hill, drawing nearer by the second.

'You're the primary person of interest, Kyle. I wouldn't plan on getting much sleep anytime soon.'

Kyle sighed, folded his hands behind his head. 'Sleep is overrated. I just hope Forsyth has plenty of tea available.'

Chapter Twenty-Eight

'It was something Rebecca Wilson told you?' DI Forsyth's expression telegraphed his utter disbelief.

'That's right,' Kyle said. 'She mentioned South Weald, some childhood connection. A place where she felt safe, I think was the phrase she used. Not much to go on, but I thought it might be worth exploring.'

'Sounds pretty thin to me. Tell me the truth. What were you doing in South Weald?'

'Like I said, looking for Rebecca.'

'And Kenneth Munday.'

'Not specifically, no. I don't actually care about Kenneth Munday. He's the Met's problem, not mine.'

Forsyth adopted a cynical expression. 'Was Kenneth Munday there?'

'If he was, he was keeping a pretty low profile.' Which wasn't far from the truth.

The interview room smelled of stale smoke, old sweat. The blinds on the single locked window were filthy with accumulated dust and mould. The grey light of dawn was beginning to filter through the gaps, emphasising the jaundiced pallor of Forsyth's complexion. His thin moustache bore traces of grey and yellow, sure signs of premature ageing and regular nicotine abuse.

Forsyth leaned forward. 'I don't mind how long we stay

here, Kyle. I have all the time in the world.'

'I wish I could say the same.'

'I could book you f–'

'Come on, you have *nothing* on me,' Kyle interrupted. 'I called it in. Your colleague responded, and we've explained what we found.'

'A dead man who happens to be the main suspect in a murder case – the murder of a serving police officer, no less, which took place in your flat.'

Kyle shrugged. 'Someone got to him before you. Not my problem.'

'And yet we only have your word that Sven Jörgensen was alive when you called DC Bates. And these other men – of whom there is no trace.' Forsyth folded his arms. 'You expect me to believe they just vanished?'

'Whoever killed Jörgensen knows what happened. DC Bates was doing her duty; sticking close to me until backup arrived. You wouldn't have had her facing Jörgensen and co on her own, would you? Textbook stuff, Forsyth.'

'Did you kill Sven Jörgensen?'

'You're not listening.'

'You have motive. Jörgensen nicked your girl.'

Kyle shook his head. 'Not true. We finished. She met Jörgensen months later.'

'Jealousy is a powerful motive, Kyle.'

'You're wasting your time – and mine. Not that I have much on at the moment, so like I said, it's up to you how long you want to spend rattling around this dead end.'

'Describe the men Jörgensen had with him.'

Kyle groaned. 'Eastern European lorry drivers, or night club bouncers, maybe. Typical meat-for-hire.'

'Distinguishing features?'

'A startling lack of intelligence?'

'Don't screw me about, Kyle.' Forsyth flicked his teacup with his thumbnail in an irritated rhythm.

'It was dark. I wasn't looking to date any of them.'

Forsyth narrowed his eyes.

Kyle sighed. 'OK, let's see. One had a scar running down one cheek. All had short, cropped hair. One had a busted nose. The last one I dealt with had a tattoo.' As he spoke, something clicked. The tattoo, Jörgensen's wound...

Forsyth leaned forward. 'What? You've remembered something. What is it?'

The tattoo. It struck a distant chord, a faint memory. A brutal murder in a Thameside warehouse a while back. Never solved. But the clue, the only clue, had been that the dead man had had a distinctive tattoo, freshly inked on his forearm.

A stiletto.

'Spit it out, Kyle.'

He remembered Forsyth, came back to the present. 'Yes, sorry. Their English was very basic.'

Forsyth frowned. The thumbnail tapping was arrhythmic now. 'That's *it*?'

'Yep.'

'Cobblers.'

'DI Forsyth, I can't tell you any more. That's all I've got.' Kyle began to whistle the opening bars of Cliff Richard's *Congratulations*.

Forsyth looked at his watch. 'Whistle all you like, Kyle. I can keep you here for a further twenty-one hours, should I so choose.'

'Choose away. What shall we talk about?'

Forsyth pushed his chair back so violently it clattered to the floor. The duty PC glanced over, shot Kyle a sympathetic look.

Forsyth was on his feet, ranting. Kyle closed his ears.

The door opened and closed as Forsyth, along with the PC, left the room and Kyle to his thoughts.

He sipped at the cup of water Forsyth had grudgingly provided. Tea would have been nice, but it could wait.

Chapter Twenty-Nine

The Italian had them brought to his office. The four men looked disgruntled, unhappy. Heads down, they stood with their arms hanging loosely, avoiding each other's gaze. Their body language told him all he needed to know.

'Gentlemen,' he began. 'I find myself a little disappointed.' He rose from his bureau, walked slowly to the fireplace, picked up an ornamental vase and turned it over in his hand admiringly. It was a beautiful object, a piece he had found at an auctioneer's in Covent Garden. Eighteenth century, German; the thin porcelain was decorated with an encircling floral motif with a central convex masked figure. He held it up.

'Beautiful, no? One of the very first pieces produced at Meissen. The whiteness, the translucency. That is what caught my eye. The purity, the simplicity of design.'

The four men shuffled their feet. One grunted.

'The clean lines, the understatement. An object of perfection.' He placed the vase carefully back in its place. 'As you are no doubt aware, perfection is my ... watchword – is this the correct idiom?' He raised his eyebrows. 'Ah, but your English is poor. Forgive me.' He tapped his fingernail on the mantelpiece. 'No doubt you are aware that I had to ... let the original team go – your predecessors, *capisci*? They were underperforming. You were brought in to replace them. And yet…' the Italian spread his hands, 'here we are again, facing imperfections. It is most … upsetting.'

One of the men, the bullet-headed one with the green shirt spoke up. 'We didn't know Jörgensen was being tailed.'

'No?' The Italian made a face. 'But you were busy, yes? A little distracted, perhaps? Well, it is understandable, of course.'

The atmosphere lifted fractionally. One of the men grinned at another.

'So, a summary, perhaps.' The Italian moved to the window, his back to the room. 'Mr Jörgensen persuades you to help him, and you agree. I imagine he proposes a generous reward, yes?' He turned elegantly to face them. 'But there is a problem. Mr Munday is not stupid – a charge I might reasonably level at yourselves.'

The man who'd grinned narrowed his eyes.

The Italian noted the change and continued. 'No, Mr Munday knows that Mr Jörgensen has already made a decision to work for himself, to the exclusion of other … interested parties, myself included. Mr Munday is waiting for you, and he has brought a friend. A large friend who then takes each of you in turn. And before you know it, you are behind a barred door waiting for *la polizia* to arrive, mm?'

'Jörgensen told us to search. We were not expecting trouble,' one of the men volunteered.

The Italian raised his forefinger. 'But there *was* trouble, was there not? There is a lesson here for you, I think. *Always* expect trouble. *Always*. And then you will not be surprised when it … turns up, yes?' The Italian looked pleased. 'And now the money has gone away with Mr Munday and his female friend – money that rightfully belongs to me, but which Mr Munday has declined to hand over.'

'And so I ask myself these questions: who is this large fellow? Where has he come from? What is his interest? And I find that he has been a policeman, and Mr Munday has struck up a liaison with this ex-policeman's friend, a woman. The same woman who has sprung – is this correct? – *sprung* Mr Munday from his incarceration.'

Blank faces.

'Gentlemen, I do not take kindly to interference. I do not take kindly to disloyalty. Nor do I accept failure.'

The spokesman moistened his lips. His face still bore traces of heavy bruising. 'We are willing to put the matter right for you. We will try again.'

The spokesman's friends nodded. One made a clenched fist gesture.

'Try?' The Italian considered the proposition. 'No, no. You misunderstand me. You will not try. You will achieve.'

The spokesman nodded.

'But you are four,' the Italian said, walking towards the group. 'Four, I think, is too many. Too clumsy. I think we will have three. We will have a *streamlining*.'

The spokesman looked confused. 'But we–'

The Italian slipped his hand inside his jacket. When it reappeared it was holding a lightweight Beretta. The spokesman held up his hand in an attempt at defence, but the bullet punched through the flesh of his palm and into his chest. He sank slowly to the floor.

The Italian went to his desk and pressed a buzzer. 'May I please request a removal? *Grazie.*'

Moments later the door opened and two men in overalls came in. One took the spokesman's arms, the other his legs, and between them they carried the corpse out of the room.

The three remaining men were silent.

The Italian bent, examined the oiled oak flooring. He went to his desk a second time, pressed the intercom button. 'Roseanne? A bucket, please, warm water. And a cloth. *Andiamo.*'

He returned his attention to the three remaining men, waved both hands dismissively, as if shooing away a wasp or mosquito. 'Go, go. *Arrivederci.* I will contact you. Very soon.'

Chapter Thirty

Kyle threw the London A to Z on the coffee table and looked at his watch. An hour till his hospital appointment. Bates would just have to keep trying if he wasn't in. And she would keep trying, of that he was confident.

He felt better today, just twenty-eight hours since DI Forsyth had let him go. A decent night's sleep in his own bed, a headache at the lower end of the scale and several cups of carefully brewed tea had all played their part in counteracting the effects of his lost night's sleep.

He went through to the kitchen, tried to second-guess Benjamin's questions. 'Been taking it easy, Mr Kyle? Headaches still troubling you? Any dizziness, vertigo, nausea? How are you sleeping? No contact sports activity, I hope?' And the prognosis, as inconclusive as before. 'We'll have to see how things go, Mr Kyle. If you experience any symptomatic changes, the rule of thumb is: straight to Casualty, understood? No messing around. There won't be time for that. I'll make sure your case notes are on hand for the staff. I'm sure they'll do their absolute best if … should the worst come to the worst.'

A handshake, a sympathetic, tight-lipped smile, end of consultation. A tick in his patient file.

Kyle took a mouthful of breakfast cereal. This one tasted of doughnuts, which was odd as its main ingredient was wheat.

... should the worst come to the worst...

There was clearly nothing to be done. His choice was no choice at all; he simply had to live day by day until *the* day came. And how would that day begin? Normally? With an 8/10 headache, or maybe no headache at all? Would there be any clue that the sliver of bullet inside his head had moved closer to some vital spot? Or would it just be total blackout, here one moment, gone the next?

Too much time alone, Kyle. Never a good idea ... Way too much thinking time...

The jangling of the telephone saved him from further introspection. He dumped his mug in the sink, went to answer.

'Ah. You *are* there.'

'I was thinking.'

'Good thoughts, I hope?'

Kyle smiled. Bates sounded upbeat; He was glad things had worked out for her. 'Since you ask, I was just wondering what to do with the rest of my indeterminate life span.'

Bates made an irritated noise, not quite a splutter, more of a *tch*. 'Aren't we all in the same place, Kyle? No one knows when their time is up. None of us. You just have to keep going, make plans, assume everything will be all right – well, bearable, anyway.'

'Wow. Deep philosophy at this hour of the morning.'

Bates laughed. 'Best I can come up with at short notice. Listen, I have the info you wanted.'

'Fire away.'

'Munday had quite a few female love-interests, it seems, but a name that crops up in his files most often is one

Jacqueline Gower. Her address has changed several times over the last five years, but I followed the trail, and with a little help from the GPO, it led me to her new address.'

'London?'

'Oh, yeah.'

'And not a million miles from HMP Fairview?'

'Correct. You'll love the next bit.'

'I can't wait.'

Bates clucked her tongue. 'She moved to number 12 Weald Rise six months ago.'

'There you go.'

'Could just be coincidence?'

'You don't believe that any more than I do, DC Bates. I'm guessing you haven't shared this with DI Forsyth.'

'You guess right.'

'And you're still content to leave it alone.'

'That wasn't a question, was it?'

'It wasn't, no.'

Bates sighed. 'What good will banging him up again do?'

'My point exactly.'

Bates lowered her voice. 'But … I can't believe I'm burying this. Do you know what would happen to me if anyone found out?' Her voice ended in a whisper. 'My God, Kyle, I hope no one's tapping this line.'

'You've been reading too many Ian Fleming novels.' Kyle adopted an exaggerated Michael Caine Cockney accent. 'Listen, darlin', the Met ain't that sophisticated, trust me.'

He heard the smile in her reply. 'I hope you're right. Anyway, I don't want to talk about it any more on the phone – or ever, actually.'

'Fine by me.'

Bates was quiet for a moment. 'But what are you going to do?'

'Do? Nothing.'

'You expect me to believe that?'

'I just like to know, that's all.'

Bates exhaled. 'OK. Look, I have to go. I'm late for a meeting.'

'Thanks for calling.'

'I'd say my pleasure, but I'd be lying.'

'See you around, DC Bates.'

'Sure. Bye, Kyle.'

The line went dead. Kyle replaced the receiver stood quietly for a while, thinking.

A lorry honked its horn outside, jolting him from his reverie. He looked at his watch. If he left now he'd just make his appointment. He found his jacket and headed for the front door, checked himself, backtracked to the lounge and picked up the A to Z, slipped it into his pocket and went out.

Chapter Thirty-One

Kyle left the hospital with mixed emotions. Benjamin had waxed eloquent regarding advances in both nuclear medicine and, in particular, cranial ultrasound, all of which was so much gobbledegook to Kyle. The bottom line seemed to be that, in time, the precise nature of Kyle's brain injury could be evaluated more accurately.

Kyle wasn't holding his breath. Even if they could see more clearly what was going on in his brain, the necessary invasive medical techniques required to fix him would probably take years rather than months to evolve. And by then ... well, who could say where – if anywhere – he would be?

He sat on a bench outside the hospital, opened the A to Z, found Fairview's page and scanned the street names. There were a number of Weald Rises, but Bates' Weald Rise was there in black and white, half way down. If he caught a bus, he could be there in, what, twenty minutes?

Without any clear idea of his motive he found himself waiting at a bus stop and boarding the first double-decker that came along. The bus stopped every few hundred yards, or so it seemed to Kyle, and the journey took much longer than his anticipated twenty minutes. When he eventually disembarked, the local school was coming out and the pavements were busy with gaggles of noisy, uniformed South

163

London school kids and their parents.

Kyle picked his way through them to the corner of Weald Rise and Burntwood Avenue. Half-way along Weald Rise a cement lorry was reversing out of someone's drive. He began to walk towards it, curious now to see what he had half-expected to find in or around number 12. The post-school bustle gave him enough cover to loiter outside and take a good look without attracting attention.

Number 12 was a semi-detached, set plumb in the middle of a well-to-do, professional area. Good catchment for the local schools, neighbours who'd be trustworthy enough to keep a spare key for you. Stockbroker land, in a nutshell. It was pretty obvious that a building project was in the throes of near-completion at the property; the drive was partially covered with a mixture of ground-in sand and cement dust, and two empty pallets were stacked by a flower bed, the corner of which was scored by wide tyre tracks, probably the result of careless reversing by some hungover JCB operator.

Kyle examined the house frontage. Unless all the work had been carried out at the rear of the property there was no indication that any building improvements had taken place at all. Attic conversion, possibly? Keeping up with the trend that was becoming more and more popular these days?

Or maybe the basement...

More likely, given Munday's history of long seclusion. Secure, enclosed; home from home, with added benefits.

Kyle approached the front door, knocked.

When the door was opened, it was by an attractive brunette in her mid-forties. Her blouse was unbuttoned to the point where the swell of her breasts drew the eye downwards towards her slim waist and elegant legs. Her skirt was fashionably short – these days they were getting shorter by the month – and her shoes looked expensive. Did she look like a businesswoman? A married woman?

A *kept* woman?

'Hello. I was just passing,' Kyle said with a cheery grin. 'I couldn't help noticing your chestnut could do with pollarding. I'm surprised the builders didn't catch the branches with their equipment.'

'You from the arboretum Samaritans then, love?'

Kyle laughed politely. 'No, but my company specialises in pollarding, stump removal – anything to do with trees, really.'

'Sorry, darlin'. Not today.'

The door was closing. 'The roots can be a problem,' Kyle said quickly. 'Especially at basement level.'

The door opened again. 'Is that so? Builders never said nothing.'

'Well, it's probably not their specialty. You've had the basement renovated?'

'You're keen, I'll give you that.'

'As I said, I was just passing…'

'Copper, are you?'

Kyle's words froze in his mouth. She might look like a Hollywood queen, but she was no fool. She was looking at him, sizing him up.

'You're on your own, love, aren't you? Following a hunch, I'd say. Well, let me tell you, there's nothing to see here.'

'I *used* to be a policeman,' Kyle admitted. 'I'm … retired.'

'You should have stuck to it, love. You're good.' She folded her arms. 'This is for your ears alone, all right? He was *supposed* to have been 'ere, yes. But he's not. He's found an … alternative…'

'I see.'

'Well, I bloody don't. Still, what can you expect? You make plans, you trust people, don't you? And then…' She shrugged. 'They crap on you.'

'If you hear anything…'

She interrupted with a guffaw. 'I'll not. And neither will you. When he wants to disappear, he does. He's damn good at it.'

Kyle nodded. There was nothing to add.

'Appreciate your discretion, love,' she said. 'No one likes being taken for a fool, and I'm no exception.'

'I … understand your frustration, believe me,' Kyle said. 'I hope you'll find a use for your … basement conversion.'

'I'll get myself a tenant, love. At least I'll make a bit of money.'

'Yes. Yes, I suppose so.'

'Nice to chat – I wouldn't mind if you fancied dropping in with a brochure sometime.' She gave him a pantomime wink and closed the door.

As Kyle retraced his steps to the bus stop it began to rain, but the drops fell on his bare head unheeded. Lost in thought, his feet slapped on the wet paving stones as he turned over the events of the past few days in his mind, and was left wondering who was the bigger fool.

Chapter Thirty-Two

That evening Kyle sat in semi-darkness nursing a Metaxa – as the bottle was open – and pondering his motive for visiting Weald Rise. The reason, he concluded, was multi-faceted. Sure, he'd wanted to know how Rebecca fitted into Munday's schemes, and he now had an answer to that; Rebecca had caused Munday to abandon his carefully prepared bolt hole, along with his patiently waiting ex-*amour*.

But he also wanted to know Munday's whereabouts – or rather, Rebecca's. He wanted to know how things were going to work out for her now that she was associated with a criminal on the run. Would they leave the country? Find a secluded croft in the Scottish Highlands? Surely there was nowhere in the UK that Munday could go without arousing at least some suspicion. Kyle thought of Ronnie Biggs, the Great Train Robber, thought to have fled to Australia. Was that Rebecca's intended destination? To Kyle, it all seemed wildly fantastical, and everything boiled down to one simple question:

Was that *really* what Rebecca wanted?

The doorbell rang.

Nine o'clock. Who called round at nine? Kyle levered himself upright and went to find out.

'Sorry. Are you busy?' In stark contrast to her usual work jacket and skirt, DC Bates was wearing a long-sleeved, loosely-belted navy dress with large pearl buttons down the front. Her hair was unclipped, swept back and held away from her forehead by a matching Alice band. She looked stunning.

'Not at all.' Kyle found his voice. 'Come in.'

Bates walked past him and Kyle shut the door. The scent of her perfume lingered in the hallway. He followed her into the lounge, embarrassed at the dirty plate, half-empty mug and scattered newspapers.

'Sorry about the mess. Look, I'm surprised you want to be here again, after—'

'Dad always told me to face my fears.'

Kyle nodded. Daughters and dads, the closest bond. 'Drink?'

'Anything.' She paused. 'Maybe not Metax– what was that stuff called?'

'Metaxa.'

'Right. Not that.'

'Of course.'

Kyle found a can of unopened lager and mixed Bates a lager and lime in a tumbler. He took the Metaxa bottle through on a tray, set it down and gave her the tumbler.

'Thanks. What about you? You don't mind being here when someone died on your sofa?'

'Doesn't bother me. I've seen worse.'

'I'll bet.' She sipped her lager. 'Forensics tidied everything up all right?'

'I've no cause for complaint.' Kyle eyed the Metaxa bottle, played with his empty glass, ran his finger around the rim. 'How's the investigation?'

'Which one? Munday, or—'

Kyle's expression made the question superfluous.

Bates traced the carpet pattern with her shoe.

'You can sit down, you know.'

She nodded, chose an armchair. 'Forsyth's not stupid. The fingerprints on the letter opener are conclusive, but I know he's still thinking about it.'

'Is that why you're here?'

A shrug. 'I don't know. I can't stop thinking about what happened. I can't sleep. I can't relax.'

'It wasn't your fault.'

'Maybe not, but still—'

'I know how it feels to have something hanging over you.' Kyle stretched across and poured himself a finger of Metaxa.

Bates adopted a crestfallen expression. 'Of course you do. I'm being insensitive. Your injury – I wasn't thinking...'

'No, it's not that. It's the fact that I could have done something to prevent Colin's – my friend's – death. But I didn't.' He was aware that the Metaxa was beginning to loosen his tongue, but there was something about Bates that invited openness.

'*If onlys* are a poor way to review the past, Kyle. As an ex-copper you should know that.'

'I do. But...'

'It's human nature. I get it.'

'But you're at it as well.'

Bates gave a self-disparaging laugh. 'Yes. If only I'd said something, spoken to someone about Patterson. It needn't have come to ... what it came to.'

Kyle noticed her nervous glance at the sofa. If he half-closed his eyes he could still see the ghostly outline of

Patterson's lifeless body on the sofa, the uninvited guest.

He was about to change the subject when Bates said, 'So, you and Rebecca Wilson. Were you together long?'

'Just under a year.' Kyle felt strangely encouraged by the question.

'And you think she and Munday, they're…'

'It certainly appeared so.'

'I was thinking, it's an odd thing to happen. I mean, I get it that some women have a thing for older men, but—'

'He's a charmer, our Munday. Rebecca and he spent a lot of time together. I'm sure she didn't take him on as a client in the hope that they might form a relationship.' He shrugged. 'These things happen.'

'You went to Weald Rise, didn't you?'

Kyle stood up, went to the bay window and drew the curtains. Outside the rain was falling in a steady downpour. 'Yes.'

'And?'

'He wasn't there. I was reliably informed that his plans had changed.'

'By Jacqueline Gower, I presume?'

Kyle nodded. 'Not a happy bunny.'

Bates looked thoughtful. 'I'll bet. If Forsyth finds out, he'll have her in for questioning before you can say *Double Diamond works wonders*.'

'But he's not going to find out, is he?' Kyle gave Bates a hard stare. 'You're not on some "honesty is the best policy" crusade, are you?'

'No. I'm just saying.'

'I doubt whether Gower knows anything anyway.' Kyle glanced at his watch. 'Look, how about a change of scenery?

Fancy a drink at the local? It's not too bad.'

'Sure, why not?'

As they left the flat, Kyle slid his arm around Bates' slender waist. They ducked their heads against the gusting rain and half-walked, half-ran down the street and into the warm and fuggy embrace of the Red Lion's saloon bar. They shouldered their way to the bar and, as Kyle tilted his chin to attract the barmaid's attention, he felt Bates' hand slip easily into his.

Chapter Thirty-Three

The bell rang. 'Last orders, let's be *havin'* 'ew … thank 'ew kindly, ladies and gentle*men*.'

Kyle had secured a corner table and had a good view of the pub interior. He felt safer with his back to the wall. Old habits…

'What are you thinking?' Bates reached across the table and squeezed his hand.

'Oh, nothing. This, I suppose. Us. I wasn't–'

'Neither was I, Kyle.' She smiled, sipped her Babycham.

The crowded bar was thinning. The combination of Metaxa and bitter had produced a pleasantly soporific effect. No headache, a pretty girl, a new start.

Through his relaxed haze he became aware that someone was looking in their direction, a familiar face. Recognition kicked in, his mood darkened and his perceptions sharpened. The man was making his way towards them through the knots of late drinkers towards them.

'Look out,' Kyle warned. 'Sherlock approaching.'

Bates followed his gaze. 'Oh, God.'

'Well, well, well. Good evening, both. Business or pleasure, DC Bates?'

'Evening, sir.' Bates had stiffened, folded her arms, declined to answer the question.

DI Forsyth looked at each of them in turn. 'Bit of both,

maybe, eh?' He grinned, lit a cigarette, blew smoke. 'Fancy bumping into you here.'

'So is it business or pleasure for you, sir?' Bates raised her chin, po-faced.

'The former,' Forsyth answered. 'You know me, DC Bates. They call us *workaholics* these days.'

'Good to see you're backing Britain, Forsyth. The PM'll be delighted.'

Forsyth ignored Kyle's remark, eyed a spare chair at the next table. 'Mind if I join you?'

'Be my guest,' Kyle invited. 'We're not staying long.'

'No?' Forsyth drew up the chair, settled back and regarded them both again, a conspiratorial smile playing about his lips. He flicked ash into the plastic *Watneys Red Barrel* ashtray. 'Since you ask, I popped in for a chat with one of my favourite narks.'

'Oh yes?' Kyle feigned disinterest.

Forsyth leaned in. 'Yes, and do you know what, Mr Kyle? He reckons he saw no other than everyone's favourite escapee, Ken Munday, not two days ago. Guess where?'

'No idea,' Kyle said.

'Outside your block of flats, that's where.'

Kyle's brain switched reluctantly from neutral into a cautious second. 'I doubt—'

'Do you, do you?' Forsyth puffed at his cigarette. 'Good man, my snout. Rarely wrong.'

'This would be the day…' Bates began.

'Aha. *Exactly.* The day your old boss met his untimely end, DC Bates. Coincidence, maybe?' Forsyth looked pleased. He stubbed his cigarette out in the ash tray. 'Filthy habit. They'll ban it one day, that's my guess.' He folded his arms. 'Now, you wouldn't have run into Mr Munday, by some small chance, Mr Kyle?'

'Absolutely not.'

'Or the lovely Ms Wilson?'

'Nope.' Kyle shook his head, drained his beer. 'Sorry.'

'No need to apologise. I'm sure I can put the pieces together myself.' He looked pointedly at Bates. 'With a little help from my glamorous assistant. Eight sharp tomorrow suit you, DC Bates?'

'Sir.' Bates looked at her empty glass.

The final bell to signal closure rang and the pub's clientele began to make their way to the exit in twos and threes, bracing themselves for the dash to bus stops or nearby homes. In spite of the barmaid's efforts there was still a group of older men chatting noisily at the bar. The landlord raised his voice, picked a few well-used phrases to encourage them. Laughing and joking, the men returned their beer mugs and began to file out.

Forsyth stood up. 'Well, I won't keep you. Nice to chat.' He beamed. 'Oh, one thing. I almost forgot.' He had to raise his voice to be heard. 'You've reason to recall the events of the twelfth of December last year, Mr Kyle?'

The date was firmly etched in Kyle's DNA. The twelfth of December. The day of the bullet, the day of Colin's death.

'DI Patterson always speculated that the brains behind the operation you were staking out that night was probably working from inside – making his moves in the outside world through a proxy, calling the shots like he was playing a game of chess, you might say.'

Forsyth paused, no doubt for effect. Kyle wasn't going to give him the satisfaction of a prompt, so he just waited for what was coming – although, if Forsyth's self-satisfied expression was anything to go by, it wasn't hard to guess.

The DI dutifully delivered his punch line. 'I've recently received information from a reliable source that points the finger at the aforementioned Kenneth Munday.'

'Interesting.' Kyle gripped his empty beer mug.

'Very. So … if you happen to hear anything, Mr Kyle, I'd be awfully grateful. Good night both.' He made eye contact with Bates. 'Eight sharp, mind.'

They watched him depart across the emptying room.

Bates said, 'I reckon that was a big, fat carrot.'

'Tell it to the rabbit.' Kyle stared daggers at Forsyth's retreating back.

'I told you. He's suspicious.'

Kyle said. 'He's been watching me – us. All that stuff about narks. Rubbish.'

'So he's fishing?'

'He has *nothing*. What he *does* have is a fat piece of evidence that the late Mr Jörgensen killed DI Patterson. He's just guessing that Rebecca might have confided in me regarding Munday's likely whereabouts.'

Bates said nothing for a few moments, then, 'Kyle?'

'What?'

'I was having a nice evening.' She smiled.

'Likewise.'

'I'd better get home. Early start.'

The landlord was watching them, weighing up whether or not they needed further encouragement.

Kyle acknowledged him with a wave. 'I'll walk you to your car.'

'No need.' Bates smiled at him again. 'I'm a police officer, remember? I can take care of myself.'

Chapter Thirty-Four

Kyle couldn't sleep. When he closed his eyes, all he could see was Forsyth's taunting face. Was it a lie? Had Munday been behind Colin's death? If so, it changed everything. He'd been content to let Munday get on with his life, especially with the new Rebecca connection. Who was he to interfere? But now...

He rolled onto his back, folded his arms behind his head, stared at the empty ceiling. If Munday was responsible, he had to be answerable. Kyle knew that Munday had still been able to pull strings from Fairview. They *all* could, the experienced criminals. They all had outside contacts, and there was always a compliant and bribable screw available to assist. So it was possible. Munday could have arranged the meeting that night, could have set the rules.

Any interruptions from our friends in blue, you know what to do...

And yet it didn't square with what Kyle had learned about the man in recent days. Munday wasn't afraid to use violence where necessary, but only against those he deemed deserved it. And by Kyle's reckoning, two unarmed detectives hardly fitted the bill. Unless he was very much mistaken in the man, Munday would never have sanctioned the shooting of an unarmed detective in cold blood.

So Forsyth was lying.

Keep thinking, bud, Colin-in-his-head piped up.

177

Maybe somewhere between the lies and rumours there was a grain of truth. There usually was.

Kyle swung his legs out of bed, gingerly raised his head. No worse. He got up, went through to the lounge. Patterson's outline was still on the sofa. Kyle wondered how long it would linger.

He spoke aloud. 'Who's responsible, Patterson?'

The image faded. He rubbed his eyes.

If not Munday, then who? Same organised crime gang, same MO. In Munday's absence, who might have stepped up to the plate? Who might have assumed control? Someone clever, adept at lurking in the shadows. Someone whose profile was as low as it could be.

Kyle recalled his sudden jolt of memory during Forsyth's questioning in the interview room. The warehouse murder. There'd been a great deal of speculation; a gang had had a falling out, one of their own turning on another, or maybe someone had broken in and tried to steal something.

Maybe.

Whatever, the unfortunate victim had been killed in the process, and he had never been identified. He had no connection with the legitimate owner of the warehouse, and no one had come forward to report him as missing; the only identifying mark on the body had been the fresh tattoo. The stiletto.

The weapon that had killed him.

And Jörgensen.

A stiletto.

Only one person could provide an answer. The more Kyle thought about it, the more certain he was. Ken Munday would know who was responsible; it *had* to be either Munday himself or his faceless replacement.

But to get an answer he had to find Munday.

And that wasn't going to be easy.

Kyle stirred his tea and took another sip. He'd given up the sleep thing at six. Rain beat against the kitchen window in sporadic gusts; April was living up to its reputation. His head felt heavy from sleeplessness but the headache had receded to a background throb. A two or a three.

As the caffeine did its work he went through a list of options. It wasn't a long list; in fact, there was only one item he considered worth pursuing.

Rebecca and he had been together long enough to accumulate the usual flotsam and jetsam of everyday life. Letters, wedding invitations, Christmas cards, keepsakes, shared bills, certificates, books, magazines … Kyle had cleared the flat the day after Bec had left, dumped as much of their shared detritus as would fit into two suitcases and hoisted them above the wardrobe. Every knick knack, every reminder of their life together was stored in the suitcases. Munday might be difficult to find, but maybe, just maybe, Bec would be a little easier. There might be *something*, an indication, a tiny clue as to where she – they – might have gone. In every relationship, if the man had any sense he would always be wise to heed a woman's instinct regarding a potential home.

Munday had sense.

Rebecca had the instinct.

Kyle sipped his tea. The radio was tuned to Radio One, the volume low. Tom Jones was singing at full throttle:

I felt the knife in my hand…

Kyle turned the set off with an irritated flick. He retraced his thoughts. A woman's instinct...

Bec had chosen this flat. He hadn't been fussed either way, but she'd found it, decorated it to her liking, furnished it to her taste. There were traces of her everywhere, despite Kyle's attempts to cover them up. The wallpaper, the carpet, the kitchen utensils – all Bec. If he'd been in better health, perhaps he'd have moved out by now, left it all behind. But he hadn't, and the reminders of her presence were still very much in evidence. He tried to remember conversations they'd had about life, living, moving to new places.

Holidays, dreams, aspirations...

He finished his tea and went into the bedroom. The first suitcase was lighter than he'd remembered; papers, mainly. He placed it on the bed and undid the locks.

Each item was a memory. A birthday card, a love note. A restaurant receipt. A catalogue of good times. After ten minutes he was finding it hard, but he made himself carry on sifting, checking, remembering. His eyes became blurry, and still he carried on.

He was almost at the bottom of the suitcase, just a few scraps left when his hand fell on a photograph. It was a postcard-sized image of a semi-derelict cottage. Kyle studied it. Bec had talked about it; he dredged through his memory, finally recalling that the cottage had belonged to a family member, one of Bec's aunts on her mother's side. Welsh? That rang a bell.

He peered at the photograph. The name of the cottage was inscribed in faded print at the bottom. He fetched a magnifying glass, and the letters swam into focus.

Goitre Bach, Tywi.

Now he remembered. Bec's aunt had died, leaving the cottage unoccupied. Her mother had told Bec that her father had always expressed a desire to renovate the place, perhaps relocate there in retirement, or maybe rent it to holidaymakers during the summer. It had never happened. Kyle retrieved his bundle of Ordnance Survey maps from a drawer, spread the appropriate map on the bed. There was Tywi, an area of conifer forest near Tregaron. As isolated as you could wish for. One of the more remote parts of Mid-Wales.

Perfect, in fact.

The phone rang. Kyle went impatiently to answer it.

'Morning. I just wondered how you were.'

'I know where they are,' Kyle said.

Bates took a moment to respond. Kyle listened to her breathing.

'I'm coming with you.'

Kyle was silent.

'You're not safe on your own.'

That was probably true. 'What are you going to tell Forsyth?'

'I'll think of something.'

'He won't be happy.'

'My decision.'

Kyle thought about it, but only for a second. 'Can you be ready by midday?'

'Is the Pope a Catholic?'

This was a new one on Kyle. He laughed. 'I'll see you then.'

He replaced the receiver, still smiling.

Chapter Thirty-Five

'What makes you so certain?' Bates' forehead creased as she changed gear, eased her Austin A40, an ancient vehicle she'd christened *The Flying Flea*, a further few yards towards the traffic lights.

'I'm not. But it's a strong possibility.' He looked up from the map. 'Besides, it's all I have right now.'

'And the plan?' She threw him a glance. 'I probably need to know it.'

Kyle folded the map, took an orange from the brown bag at his feet, started peeling it. 'That might be a problem. All in good time.'

'You don't have one.'

'I've a rough idea.'

'How rough?'

Kyle offered Bates an orange segment. She'd brought the fruit with her. She'd remembered.

'No, ta. I don't want to deprive you.'

'I have an entire bag. Even I can't manage them all.'

She grinned. 'If you're sure.'

He reached over and popped a segment into her mouth. 'Maybe it'll shut you up for a bit while I think.'

'Hey! Watch it. I'm your transport, remember?'

'I'm grateful. Really I am.'

She nodded, apparently satisfied. 'It'll be late when we get there – if we get there.' She drummed on the steering wheel in frustration. The traffic was bad and getting worse.

'What did you tell Forsyth?'

'Don't worry about it.'

'I do.'

'I pulled a female issue.'

'Did you, indeed?'

'He didn't know what to say. First time I've ever seen him flustered.'

'He's not likely to be following us, then.'

'Nope.'

Kyle nodded. 'Brave. Not sure I could have done that in your shoes.'

Bates snorted. 'About time someone turned the tables. You know what it's like for a woman in the Met.'

'I do, yes. Bee was toying with the idea of joining. I put her off.'

'You don't talk about her much.'

'What's to say? She left me. That's it.'

They drove in silence for a while. Traffic began to thin the further west they travelled. The rain stopped and the sun made a brief appearance, teasingly low between the clouds, before disappearing again in a wash of grey.

'Would you have her back?' Bates asked quietly.

Kyle looked up. 'You've been mulling that over for the last ten minutes?'

'I'm just interested, that's all.'

'I don't know. It won't happen, anyway.'

'But if it did, would you?'

'Bates? Please?'

'Don't you think we should be on first-name terms by

now?'

Kyle inclined his head. 'If you prefer – I'm kind of used to Bates.'

'Well, don't mind me. If you want formal, that's fine too.'

'I've hurt your feelings. I'm sorry.'

'It's OK. I'm all right. You haven't.'

The silence that followed was tense, like the final minutes before a thunderstorm. There was electricity in the air but how much of it was positive and how much negative Kyle wasn't able to judge.

They crossed the Welsh border at eight, just as the watery sun was calling it a day. It made a valedictory appearance for a few minutes, then sank over the horizon.

'We need somewhere to stay,' Bates said, breaking the long silence. 'Or are we sleeping in the Flea?'

'Let's see what happens.'

'As a plan, Kyle, that leaves a lot to be desired.'

'I'm aware.'

But Bates wasn't satisfied. 'So, we arrive at this cottage. Let's say Munday's in. You knock on the door and force him to tell you the truth about what happened in the raid when your friend was killed. He either tells you or he doesn't. Let's say he does. Let's say he's guilty. What then? You beat him up – in front of Rebecca? Kill him?'

Kyle rubbed his eyes with the heels of his hands. 'I don't know, OK? Of *course* I won't kill him.'

'No? The doctors said you had psychopathic tendencies, yes? Unless I got that bit wrong.'

'Pull over.'

'What?'

'Pull over.'

'Why?'

'I can do this myself. I shouldn't have involved you. Pull over.'

'No.'

'*Bates!*'

Bates put her foot down and Kyle banged his head on the side window. When she realised what had happened she jammed on the brakes and brought the car to a standstill.

'I'm sorry. Your head.'

'I'm all right.' Kyle opened the door. 'Go home. Forget this.'

He stepped onto the verge, slammed the door, walked on. He heard Bates revving the engine behind him. He rubbed his forehead. No harm done.

The Flying Flea drew up alongside him. She leaned over, unwound the passenger window.

'Kyle. Get in. This is stupid. You're in the middle of nowhere.'

'I'll hitch. Go home.'

'Someone has to watch your back.'

A lorry appeared, honked its horn, sailed past inches from the A40's wing mirror.

'Drive on. You'll get shunted.' Kyle kept walking.

'Psychopathic *and* stubborn,' she yelled.

'All fine qualities for the job,' he shouted back. 'I'll be fine.'

'It's not you I'm worried about.'

A more cautious queue of traffic was beginning to build up behind Bates. Horns began to blare as she continued a slow kerb crawl.

Kyle glared. 'Move on!'

'I bet you can't speak a word of Welsh,' she said. 'I can.

My grandparents were from Aberystwyth.'

'Good for you.'

The horns were now a discordant symphony; no one could overtake due to a bend in the road ahead. Kyle's head was aching. He took a few more steps then stopped.

Bates brought the car to a halt alongside. 'Please get in, Kyle.'

The horns rose to a crescendo.

Defeated, he opened the door and sank into the passenger seat.

'See. I can be stubborn too.' Bates pulled away, changed into second.

'So it seems. Drive on before we fall victim to a lynch mob.'

'Only forty miles to go. And a bit.' Bates began to hum a tune. 'You don't have to talk to me, it's fine.'

Kyle sat quietly for a while, turning over likely scenarios in his mind. He'd catch Munday off guard, for sure. The last thing the escapee would expect was anyone showing up on his doorstep. But how would he react? Munday was no saint. They'd negotiated an uneasy truce before, but that had expired. Sure, Bec trusted the man, but Kyle never would.

Whatever happened, he would get to the truth.

He owed that much to Colin.

Chapter Thirty-Six

They arrived in Tregaron just after ten. Kyle wanted to ask for directions in the hotel, but Bates pointed out that her Welsh language skills would allay any suspicion concerning the true nature of their visit. She could spin some yarn about wanting to visit the area in the morning, do some walking, a little birdwatching. She'd heard there was a derelict cottage – she'd quite like to sketch it. It sounded plausible. Kyle conceded, agreed to wait in the car.

A few minutes after Bates had disappeared into the hotel a group of youths staggered drunkenly out of the bar, shouting and joking but they passed the Flying Flea without paying it any attention. Kyle massaged his neck muscles; they were stiff with tension.

Bates reappeared. 'All OK. They have rooms, and they'll do us a plate of sandwiches if we want. No hot food till breakfast.'

'Rooms? Now?'

Bates put her hands on her hips. 'Please tell me you're not intending to tackle Munday in this?' She gestured around her at the steadily falling rain. 'We're out in the sticks, Kyle. There's no light. You won't be able to see a damn thing. And Munday'll be prepared – we both know he will be. He'll not have left things to chance.'

Kyle grunted. He was weary after the previous night's

aborted sleep. A bed, something to eat. It sounded sensible. Tomorrow was another day and Munday, if he *was* in the vicinity, had no reason to suspect that his location had been compromised.

Face it, Kyle, you can't even be certain he's here at all …

'Come on, Kyle. I'm tired and hungry.'

The hotel foyer was as Kyle had expected to find it – drab, but warm and clean. Bates was booking them in.

'Two singles?' The clerk looked at them suspiciously.

'Please.'

'Names in the register.'

A book was pushed across the counter. The clerk, a middle-aged woman with blonde, badly permed hair, sniffed as Bates entered her name. 'Rooms on separate floors, look.' She squinted at Bates' entry. 'Yourself on the first, 101, and himself on the second, 129.' She nodded towards Kyle. He accepted the biro from Bates and scrawled his name and address.

'On holiday, is it?' The woman looked them up and down.

'Walking, sketching,' Bates shot her a smile. 'A little rest and relaxation with my cousin.'

'Cousin, is it?' The woman thawed a little, took the register back with a flourish. 'Family is important here. We like to keep everything in the family. The way God intended.'

'Absolutely.' Bates beamed.

She passed the room keys across the counter. 'If you go through to the saloon I'll get the girl to prepare you some sandwiches. Won't be much. Ham or cheese, I expect. Fresh, though. Nothing processed here.'

'Anything you can do,' Kyle said. 'We'd appreciate it. It's

been a long day.' He looked pointedly at Bates.

They found a corner table, and Kyle ordered a Coke for Bates and an orange juice for himself. The young barman was in the process of packing up for the night, but grudgingly reopened the till to take Kyle's money. The sandwiches came and Kyle ate mechanically, chewing the coarse bread with scant awareness of the filling. Neither spoke.

Bates finished first. There was an awkward silence. 'Right. I'll see you in the morning.' She stood up.

'Sure.' Kyle nodded. 'Thanks for the lift,' he added.

'No problem.' She walked away towards the stairs.

Kyle watched her go. He felt a pang of guilt that he'd involved her. And something else, too – but he didn't care to analyse that too deeply.

He sat by himself, turning over tomorrow's possible scenarios. Munday was somewhere else altogether. Or Munday was indeed in residence at *Goitre Bach*, and he would tell Kyle the whole truth. Or he wouldn't. He would probably lie – the criminal's default – but, Kyle reasoned, Munday was a different kind of criminal; there was a layer of integrity lurking somewhere beneath that hard exterior, and that was the place Kyle needed to reach. Maybe Bec would help. If Munday failed to respond to his own entreaties, perhaps she could appeal to the man's better nature.

Or maybe Munday would show his other side, the side that had earned him a long prison sentence. People like Munday were at their most dangerous when cornered, and a situation like that wouldn't end well. Kyle knew he had to approach the man cautiously, persuasively, keep any latent psychopathy well under control. Bates seemed good for him in that respect. Maybe that's why she was here. Kyle didn't believe in much, let alone in divine providence, but sometimes things just seemed to fall into place. Maybe Bates was one of those things.

He looked up as the hotel door banged open and a tall man in a long coat and expensive-looking shoes came in, removed his hat, shook the water from it and made his way across the foyer to check in. He caught Kyle's eye, nodded a polite greeting. He looked foreign. Spanish?

Or Italian, perhaps.

As Kyle made his way up to his room he wondered what might bring an Italian to a place like Tregaron. Business, most likely; there certainly didn't seem to be much pleasure on offer here.

With that thought echoing in his mind Kyle undressed, fell onto the bed and passed into a deep sleep.

Chapter Thirty-Seven

The knocking was persistent. Kyle wanted it to stop. He invited the noise into his dream, where perhaps he could control it.

He was striding through an area of dense woodland, cutting a path through a tangle of foliage. There was something behind him, something fast. He could hear it crashing through the undergrowth. He tried to walk faster, but in the way of dreams, the more he tried to pick it up, the more his pace slowed.

He looked at his feet. They were caked in mud, so much mud. That was why he couldn't go any faster. He came to an inevitable standstill as the mud assumed a weight entirely out of proportion to its volume. He was stuck fast, and his pursuer knew it.

Kyle turned to face whatever was coming. A figure appeared, darting from tree to tree. One moment it was there, the next it was somewhere entirely different, all laws of physics and geometry broken. The figure was pointing something at him. He heard four loud reports.

Four knocks.

'Kyle? It's Bates. Get up. I've seen her.'

The fog lifted, the woodland dispersed. In its place, the spartan decor of his Tregaron Hotel bedroom.

'Wait. Just a minute.' He found his feet, went groggily to

the door and opened it.

Bates was fully dressed. Her eyes performed a quick appraisal. 'You look awful.'

'Thanks. What time is it?'

'Just after seven-thirty.'

'Why didn't you wake me?'

'I just *did*.' Bates compressed her lips in an expression of frustration. 'Look, I've just seen Rebecca Wilson. If it's not her, it's a damn good likeness.'

'Where? How?'

'I was downstairs, looking for somewhere I could get a cup of tea, when I spotted her in the foyer by the cigarette machine.'

'How long?'

'Couple of minutes?'

'Wait.' Kyle ducked into the bedroom, pulled on trousers, shirt, shoes, joined Bates in the corridor. 'Let's go.'

They took the stairs two at a time, exited the hotel into the square. There were few people about, one or two early morning shoppers, a deliveryman unloading. A man with a German Shepherd on a long lead. Kyle's gaze ranged from east to west, and he pointed. 'There. By the corner.'

It was Bec, no doubt about it. He'd recognise her anywhere. As he watched she slipped into a Cortina saloon and they heard the engine cough into life.

'Did she see you?'

'She doesn't know me, Kyle.'

'Car keys?'

Bates dangled them in his face.

'Let's go.'

They pulled away from the square as the Cortina

disappeared from view. Bates was still in second gear, crawling up to a T-junction. Kyle wanted to get out and run.

'I know where she's headed.' Bates had read him like a book. 'She'll make a right turn a few hundred yards past the petrol station. I checked the map, Kyle. And I'm taking it slow so she doesn't see us, OK?'

'OK.' Kyle was still struggling to wake up.

Sure enough, the Cortina made the turn, Bates following at a discreet distance. Up ahead, a tractor pulled out in front of them and Bates eased the pressure on the accelerator.

'Hope you've got your *fancy meeting you here* speech ready.' Bates shot him a look.

'I don't do speeches.' His harsh tone bounced back at him accusingly. She didn't deserve it. 'Look, Bates–'

'Judy. My parents call me Jude.'

He nodded. 'All right … Jude … I really appreciate your going out on a limb like this.'

'Don't mention it.' She pointed ahead. 'Hello … tractor's turning off.'

The Cortina was still visible, threading its way along the narrow lane. Bates stepped on the gas and the Flea shot forward.

'Any time now.' Bates slowed a little as the Cortina indicated, turned left. Bates drew into the verge, parked. 'Better if we walk from here, I'd say.'

'You weren't in the Girl Guides by any chance?'

'No. Why?'

'No reason.' Kyle clambered out. He could have done with a mug of tea. His head felt thick, as though he'd been on a bender the night before. 'Look, I don't mind if you want to stay put, look after your car.'

'I've come this far.' She joined him on the verge. A tractor with an attached trailer roared past, the driver raising a casual hand in greeting.

'OK.' Kyle understood; she'd made an investment, taken a lot of risks. Nevertheless he felt responsible for her. The last time he had staked out a property … he thrust the memory aside, bent and redid his hastily-tied shoelaces, straightened up. 'It's just that things could get heated.'

'You don't say.'

'Fine.' Kyle lifted his hands in surrender. 'Don't say I didn't warn you.'

'Just remember I'm a police officer, Mr Kyle – it's in your interest to bear that in mind.'

Kyle was already walking towards the track where the Cortina had turned off. He called back. 'So you keep reminding me. I'm sure Munday will be delighted to make your acquaintance. Mind you–'

'What?'

'You're well out of your jurisdiction – in more senses than one.'

'The *heddlu*?'

'I was thinking of Forsyth, actually.'

'Stuff Forsyth.' She drew alongside him, matching his long strides.

'I have a sneaking feeling that your career in the Met might be short-lived.'

Bates navigated a large puddle, hopped back onto the verge. 'There's plenty more fish in the sea. He won't be my DI for ever.'

Kyle shrugged. 'I know: you're a policewoman. You can handle it.' He pointed. 'Here.'

To their left was a single track, just wide enough for a small vehicle. It descended in a gentle gradient between thick hedgerows on either side.

Kyle peered ahead. 'There's a stream at the bottom. The cottage is next to it.'

'I know, I've—'

'—seen the map?'

Bates gave him a look, kept her peace.

Presently they reached an area of thin woodland. The path gradually widened until it disappeared altogether, and the Cortina came into view, parked alongside a recently whitewashed picket fence next to a shallow stream. A narrow bridge led across the stream to a squat, two-storey building with a slate roof. A wispy column of smoke rose into the damp morning air from the single chimney.

It was clear to both of them that no one could approach the property without being seen.

Kyle grunted. 'Looks like the direct method.' He started walking, but Bates' hand fell on his arm.

'Kyle, he'll be armed.'

He shook her off impatiently. 'He won't shoot me in front of Bec.'

'You don't know that.'

He stopped. 'You're right, I don't. But being shot is overrated. Been there, seen it, done it.' He carried on walking, although he could sense Bates' tension as she walked alongside. True, he might get shot, but he was gambling on the temporary rapport he'd built with the escapee. He only needed a few seconds' hesitation – that would be enough.

They reached the bridge over the stream, unchallenged.

There were three shallow trenches cut into the ground in front of the cottage filled with a mixture of wood and what looked like peat. A squirrel was nibbling at a nut, watching them curiously from a crabapple tree to the left of the front window. As they crossed the bridge it shot up to a higher branch and continued to observe them from its new vantage point.

Kyle was wondering whether to knock when the the cottage door opened and Rebecca filled the space. Her mouth fell open. Kyle raised his finger to his lips. She stepped back smartly and slammed the door in his face.

Kyle didn't hesitate. He put his shoulder to the wood and the door splintered, crashed open, the hinges wrested from the frame. The cottage interior was dark, full of shadow. Kyle was aware of Bates just behind him. Someone was sitting in an armchair by the fireplace. Kyle blinked. Bec was standing behind the chair, her hands on the occupant's shoulders.

'I've only just fixed those bloody hinges.' Munday made no attempt to rise. He looked comfortable, unfazed by the sudden intrusion – but that was probably because he was cradling a shotgun, the twin barrels pointing directly at Kyle's chest.

Chapter Thirty-Eight

'A little early for visitors.' Munday's grip was steady on the shotgun. 'I see you've brought a friend. What's the plan? Is this the big citizen's arrest?'

The interior of the cottage smelled of fresh paint and woodsmoke. There was a narrow oak table by the window, laid for breakfast.

Kyle bunched his fists. 'Tell me the truth. No skating around.'

'Ah, a seeker after truth.' Munday nodded. 'Admirable.' He angled the shotgun a fraction to Kyle's right until it was pointing at Bates.

'Put the gun down.' Kyle felt a red mist descend. His pulse was pounding in his temple.

Munday pursed his lips. 'Can I be sure you'll behave? Perhaps an appeal from your colleague?'

'Kyle…' Bates' whisper was laced with tension.

Kyle acknowledged her warning with a dismissive gesture. 'Put it down, Munday. I don't talk to a loaded gun.'

'You're a trespasser, Mr Kyle. I could have you arrested.' Munday looked amused.

Kyle shook his head. 'You're unbelievable.'

Munday's gaze fell on Bates. 'What do you think, Ms…?'

'Bates. DC Bates.'

'A police officer? A detective?'

Munday's attention was momentarily diverted. Kyle focused on the shotgun; the twin barrels had drifted to point towards the space between him and Bates. But it was still a shotgun; the spread of the blast would take them both out. He felt sweat break out on his brow, and the throbbing in his temple intensified. It was a necessary risk. While Munday had the gun, he was in charge. Kyle judged his moment, stepped to one side and grabbed the barrels with both hands, jerked the gun towards the ceiling. The firearm went off with a roar; Kyle felt the heat from the discharge on his face. Pieces of plaster fell from the ceiling, striking him on the head and shoulders. He kept hold of the shotgun, forced all his weight behind it, crushed it against Munday's neck.

'Tell me the *truth*.'

Munday was trying to force the barrel away from his windpipe. Kyle kept the pressure on, applying all his weight.

'*Kyle!*'

His red rage blurred his vision; Munday was responsible for all his misery. Kyle kept up the pressure. He was vaguely aware of a deep sound coming from his throat, a primal growl. Bates had her arms around his waist, trying to pull him back.

'*Kyle!*'

Rebecca's hands were on his arms, tugging. 'Leave him *alone!*'

Munday's face was turning blue. He was making gagging, gasping sounds, and his pupils were dilated. Kyle saw himself reflected there; it was a face he didn't recognise, the face of a twisted, snarling animal, eyes staring, nostrils flared, hair dishevelled. The face of a madman.

'*Kyle! Please! Stop!*'

Bee was sobbing, pummelling his shoulders, his head. The blows rained down but he hardly felt them.

'Please! *Please!* Don't kill him, Kyle. Please ... oh, God, don't ... Kyle ... you don't understand...' She hit him again, a token blow, her strength exhausted. 'Kyle, listen to me! He's my *father!*'

Kyle heard Bates' gasp of astonishment. *What* had Bee said? He let go of the gun. Munday took a whoop of air, his hands went to his throat and he leaned forward, gagging. Bates whipped the shotgun away, broke it.

Bee was crying. 'I was going to tell you. I didn't know how ... I didn't want to ... what could I do, Kyle?' She clutched Munday's arm. 'He's my father. What else am I supposed to have done? What else *could* I do?'

Chapter Thirty-Nine

Munday took a sip of brandy, curled his hands around the glass and inhaled the fumes. Bec had pulled over two dining chairs from the breakfast table on which Kyle and Bates were now sitting, side by side, facing Munday. Bec was perched on the arm of her father's chair, watching him anxiously.

'I should have told you, I suppose,' she said to Kyle. 'But the right moment never arrived. You see ... ' She lowered her eyes.

Kyle's sense of perspective had returned. He got it; this was obviously a tough call. 'Take your time.'

'You deserve to know what happened.' She moistened her lips. Munday patted her arm as she began. 'I was introduced to Sven Jörgensen at Fairview. I'd only had one previous client there, so it was all new to me. I had no idea at that stage that Ken was my father.' She looked at Munday as if she still didn't really believe it, paused for a moment as if to let the fact sink in, then went on. 'Jörgensen spoke to me very persuasively about his client in solitary, you see – oh, he had ulterior motives, of course, we know that now.

Anyway, Dad knew who I was. Unbeknown to me he'd been following my career for years, and one day he saw me in Fairview. I remember I was walking along one of the corridors and he was being escorted by two prison officers towards the governor's office. As we passed each other he

200

gave me a long, lingering look. I asked another warden who he was, and he told me, but I'd never heard of him. Can you imagine that? Anyway, once Dad knew I was a regular visitor he suggested to Sven during one of their legal briefings that if he could persuade me to take him on as a client, he'd cut Sven into a percentage of his ... well, his ...'

'Illicit earnings.' Kyle helped her out.

'Well, yes.' Bec took a breath. Bates was watching her intently, but also keeping a wary eye, Kyle noticed, on the window.

'As you know, Sven and I became an item. I hadn't intended it, but that's what happened. We always seemed to bump into each other. Maybe he just wanted to be able to apply more pressure so that I'd definitely take on Dad's social care, I don't know. But there it is; we got together. I eventually agreed to interview Dad, and it was during our third appointment that he told me who he was.

'I couldn't believe it. I thought it was a wind-up, but he knew things about me that it would have been impossible to fake. Stuff from my early childhood. After he and Mum were divorced, she never mentioned him. She changed our name, never let me talk about him.' Bec wiped her eye with an irritated gesture. 'And so I just ... well, I just forgot about him.' She looked at Munday who reached out and took her hand. She continued, her voice quavering. 'And of course, as soon as I knew who he was, I wanted to help him, because, because...'

'It's all right, love, it's all right.' Munday squeezed her hand.

'Because he's dying,' Bec blurted. 'He has liver cancer. He's refused treatment, and anyway it's too late. He just wanted to spend time with me before he...'

She began to sob. Kyle didn't know what to say or where to look. Bates caught his eye and winced.

Kyle gave her a few moments. Bates gave her a handkerchief.

'Sorry.' Rebecca blew her nose hard. 'I'm OK, really.'

Kyle shook his head, thought about the risks she'd taken. He found his voice eventually. 'I get it, but ... wow, Bec, you've really gone out on a limb with this one.'

'I know.' She nodded. 'Dad wanted to make sure I was OK financially, that I had everything I needed. And then bloody Sven, he...'

'Got too greedy.' Kyle blew out his cheeks. 'Not that he's bothered any more.'

'What do you mean?' Rebecca looked up. Munday offered her another handkerchief and she blew her nose again.

'You don't know. Of course you don't.' Kyle prompted Bates with a look.

'Sven Jörgensen was murdered two nights ago,' Bates told them. 'By person or persons unknown.'

'Oh my God.' Bec's shock was genuine. 'How? I mean...'

'Later,' Kyle said. 'I need to talk to your father now. I need to know about last December.'

Munday lowered his glass. 'You want the truth? Very well. You shall have it, to the best of my knowledge.'

Kyle nodded. 'I'm listening.'

Munday settled back in the chair, rested his head. 'You'll already know from our previous conversations that my tried and tested business strategy was to target those I considered deserving of my attention – well-to-do executives with questionable business ethics, ruthless entrepreneurs, and so on. It was usually straightforward enough to find a skeleton in the appropriate closet, use it to my advantage.'

'Yes.' Kyle was in no mood for long monologues. 'But let's cut to the chase. I want to know about that night, the night my partner was killed.'

'I wasn't there. You know where I was.'

'You called the shots, though, didn't you? The people in that house were acting under your instructions.'

'At that point, actually not.' Munday set down his glass. Bee offered the brandy bottle but he waved it away. 'By that stage – by the end of the year…'

'Twelfth of December. That's the date I'm interested in.'

'All right.' Munday coughed, grimaced. 'If I might have a glass of water, darling?'

Bee went to the corner sink, returned with a glass and gave it to Munday who sipped it slowly, wincing as he swallowed. After a few moments he took a deep breath and went on.

'My operation was tricky to manage from Fairview for all sorts of reasons, particularly after I was sent to solitary. And then my lawyer – the late Mr Jörgensen we've already referred to – recommended a deputy, a man with whom he'd come into contact while abroad on business. This man's credentials were impeccable, his background highly suited to the task in hand. The question was, would he be willing to adhere to the ethical stand I had always taken for future business opportunities? There was only one way to find out. We took him on, and set him to work.'

'For a while, all was well, but then I began to hear unsettling reports of how his management style was upsetting my team. His methods were harsher than mine – ruthless, that was the word used on more than one occasion.

So by the time we reached early spring that year, I had become convinced that my decision to employ him had been a mistake.

'And then came the meeting on the Twelfth of December, a Tuesday. The regular monthly get together to discuss the month ahead. Someone had tipped you off about it; I have my suspicions about that, but that's neither here nor there. The fact is that the meeting was interrupted by two police officers – you and your friend.'

Kyle was listening intently. Bates had risen from her chair and seemed interested in something outside. She stood at the window, looking out.

'Mr Kyle, you have to understand that I'd never condone, not then, not now, not ever, the use of a firearm against an officer of the law. It's beyond the remit of anyone in my employment. But sadly, on this occasion a firearm was brought into play – with tragic results.'

'Who?' Kyle leaned forward. 'A name.'

Munday drew a deep breath, exhaled painfully. 'The man in question isn't a Brit. He's an Italian – a Calabrian, to be more precise; the Italians are very picky about their regions. Not unlike the Welsh, come to think of it. That's the man responsible for the firearm discharge on the day in question: his name is Signore Mauro Carlotto.'

'Describe him.' Kyle was thinking about last night's late arrival, the man with the hat, the expensive shoes…

As Kyle listened to Munday's description, he knew.

He turned to Bates to warn her to get away from the window, but as he formed the words the whole structure – rails, grilles, jamb, sash and thickened glass – disintegrated in a ferocious hail of bullets.

Chapter Forty

Kyle's first thought was for Bates. He crawled across the debris-strewn floor to where she was lying face-down, covered in glass. She stirred as he reached her, moved her head, groaned.

'Are you hurt?'

'I'm OK.' She rolled over, crunching on the glass and rubble, and sat up. There were two deep cuts on her forehead and right cheek, several smaller lacerations on her hands, but none of the bullets had hit her.

She propped herself against the wall beside the ragged hole where the window had been. Rain pelted into the gap, soaking them both as Kyle made a grab for the shotgun Munday had slid across the floor towards him.

Munday's low armchair had saved him; two inches higher and the story would have been different. As it was the bullets had probably parted his hair, but he looked uninjured. Bec was crouched behind the armchair, scrabbling for the cartridge case in the corner of the room. She pulled it towards her, dipped her hand, slid a box across to Kyle. She made a signal with her fingers. *Two.*

Two boxes left. One shotgun. Not good enough for what was out there. He read the box label: buckshot. That was good. Better damage potential than birdshot, but Munday knew that, hence his choice of cartridge. The buckshot had a potential range of seventy yards, and that fact in itself would allow Kyle to take the fight to Carlotto.

Munday read his thoughts, nodded. Question was, how many friends had the Italian brought with him?

And were they the same friends? Kyle loaded the shotgun, snapped it shut. That might not be the worst news. Carlotto had given Jörgensen's borrowed heavies a get-out-of-gaol-free card but their South Weald experience might give Kyle an edge. No one liked to face up to an adversary who'd caused them grief before; that was simple human nature. Once bitten…

A second burst of bullets riddled the far wall.

Bates covered her head with her hands. 'How's that plan coming along, Kyle?' She ducked again as more bullets zipped through the hole, made a neat row in the opposite wall.

Munday tossed Kyle a packet of cigarettes and a box of matches. 'The three trenches,' he said. 'Light 'em up.'

Now Kyle understood the purpose of the peat-filled indentations he'd noticed on the way in. Munday hadn't skimped on his preparations. Kyle propped the shotgun against the wall, lit three cigarettes at once, puffed them until the ends glowed red-hot.

'I need a distraction,' he told Bates. 'Hold something up. Here—' he selected a thin sliver of window frame. 'Wave it around but for God's sake keep your head down.'

He crawled to the opposite end of the gap. 'After three,' he told her.

He counted. On three, Bates lifted the wood. Bullets whipped the shard out of her hand. She yelped, snatched her hand back. At the same time Kyle stuck his head up and lobbed the three cigarettes, one for each trench. It wasn't difficult – they were an easy target. He ducked down as more bullets tracked across the gap and ripped fresh splinters from the remnant of the frame. One stabbed into his forehead, drawing blood.

Smoke immediately began to rise above the artificial horizon of the window frame.

'Soaked 'em in petrol.' Munday said, deadpan.

Kyle jerked his thumb at the window hole. 'One of them'll look in presently,' he said. 'Better field of vision than coming through the door.'

'He'll just start firing,' Bates said. 'Like shooting fish in a barrel.'

'If it's the same guys we've met before, they don't score too highly on the intelligence scale,' Kyle said. 'Wait until he pokes his head through the gap, then hit him. As hard as you can.'

'Will this do?' Bates had found a poker by the hearth. 'Happy to do the honours.'

'What are *you* going to do?' Rebecca was looking at Kyle.

Kyle thought about Carlotto. 'He'll send his buddies in first. And he'll wait to see how things pan out.' Kyle looked at Munday for confirmation.

Munday nodded. 'Most likely. He a fastidious man. He won't enjoy all this outdoor rough stuff.' He shook his head. 'Not his style. And Carlotto, whatever else he might be, is nothing if not a stylish man.'

'How many, d'you reckon?' Kyle took up the shotgun.

'No more than four,' Munday replied. 'More than that, too cumbersome to manage.'

So, five against four. Not bad odds, but right now Carlotto

had the advantage. He knew where they were. Kyle said to Bates, 'Stay by the window. Be quick. You'll have a split second before he starts firing. Munday, you have a handgun, I assume?'

A pistol appeared in Munday's hand as if by magic. 'Always.'

'Good. I'll try to draw them away. There's a back door, I assume?' The smoke was getting thicker outside and the breeze was working in their favour, blowing it to the south – hopefully in Carlotto's direction. The Italian would need to adopt a cautious approach – Munday's defences had bought them some time.

'Through the kitchen,' Rebecca said. 'It's a stable door.'

'Careful back there,' Munday advised. He'd taken up a crouching position covering the window from behind the armchair. Rebecca was hunkered down behind him, her hand resting on his shoulder.

'I intend to be.'

'No, listen – there's gin traps, two of them. One by the side gate – it's covered over – and the other by the rearmost gate that leads into the field. Long grass, you won't see it.'

'Aren't they illegal?'

Munday gave him a look.

Kyle shrugged. 'Unneighbourly, but fair play under the circumstances.'

'No one's set foot in this garden for over a decade,' Munday was unrepentant. 'I wasn't anticipating a visit from the vicar.'

'Mr Kyle, Mr Munday?' A voice from somewhere outside.

'Carlotto.' Munday's mouth twisted in distaste.

'Keep him talking,' Kyle said and, keeping his head down,

made his way to the rear of the cottage where the kitchen door lay half-open.

Carlotto's voice sailed through the wrecked window. 'Let us talk together. No need for any unpleasantness.'

'Then why the shooting?' Munday yelled back.

'I apologise. My friends are a little nervous.'

'Call them off, Carlotto.'

Kyle could hear the conversation from the kitchen, a narrow room that looked out onto a small, sloping garden. A low, straggly hedge separated the garden from the adjacent field. The stable door was a blind spot; one of Carlotto's friends might be waiting for it to open. Instead Kyle selected the kitchen window as a more strategic exit and slipped out onto the weed-covered patio.

The acrid smell of burning peat filled the air. The smoke was thick, and getting thicker by the second. Kyle ran in a half crouch to a gap in the garden hedge. He stuck his head through the hole, looked for cover in the field. There wasn't much, just the boundary fence and a stile half-way along, but it would give him a better, more elevated view of the cottage and its environs, smoke allowing; at this point the cover was working both for him and against him. But Carlotto's men were unlikely to make a subtle approach – they would show themselves eventually. Kyle pushed through the hedge and made a run for it.

He reached the stile unopposed, estimated his distance from the cottage to be around two hundred feet.

He poked his head around the stile. As he'd hoped, his vantage point gave him a clear view of the front of the cottage – or it would have done if it wasn't for the smoke. Kyle squinted, looking for movement.

Without warning a heavily-built man appeared out of the haze. He was carrying an automatic rifle and moving surprisingly quickly for a man of his size. He was also weaving from side to side, making it hard to bring the shotgun to bear. It was too late; the gunman had reached the cover of the cottage. Kyle thought of Bates, crouched beneath the frame, waiting.

Then two things happened simultaneously. He heard the sound of automatic fire from the cottage, a sharp burst that cut off as quickly as it had begun, and then someone ground a cold barrel into the base of his skull, got hold of his collar and yanked him to his feet.

'Drop it,' a voice hissed in Kyle's ear. 'I am happy to find you again. Now we see how you like the same treatment, huh?'

Chapter Forty-One

Kyle dropped the shotgun but made sure it landed at his feet, half-propped on the stile, stock pointing up. He recognised the voice; it was the first South Weald guy, the bullet-headed gap-toothed gangster he'd half-strangled. Shame he hadn't finished the job.

'Turn around. I want to see your face before I finish you.'

Kyle turned. 'Nice to see you again.' It wasn't all bad – gap-tooth was pointing a revolver at his chest. Not ideal but not as lethal as an automatic weapon. 'Carlotto will rip you off – you know that, don't you?'

'He pays us good.' Gap-tooth smiled. 'And where you are going, you don't need money.'

Kyle looked past his shoulder, focused on the middle of the field. 'Let's get out of the field first,' he warned, 'unless you want to have your back-end poked by a bull.'

Gap-tooth looked momentarily confused, then relaxed his expression into a wider grin. 'Ha ha, very good. The oldest trick in your book, huh?'

'No trick.' Kyle shook his head, feigned panic, moved back a step. 'It's coming, fast. Can't you hear it?'

...A second, just one ...

Gap-tooth succumbed to the instinct of self-preservation. He half-turned to look and Kyle stepped neatly out of the revolver's line of fire, in the same motion grabbing the shotgun and discharging it as soon as his finger curled around the trigger. It blew a hole in Gap-tooth's leg, and he went down, screaming.

'Sorry, pal. Mainly sheep farming in these parts – no bull.' Kyle took his revolver and lined it up. 'Safe trip.'

Realisation dawned. Gap-tooth held his free hand up in protest. 'No ... you cannot. You are a good man, I...'

'Wrong. I'm a psychopath.' Kyle shot him in the head, then returned his attention to the cottage. A second figure had reached the back gate. He raised the shotgun, but then remembered what Munday had said. A second later a piercing scream rent the air.

He lowered the shotgun. Two down, potentially two to go – three if you counted Carlotto.

He waited.

Two, three. Five minutes.

Nothing.

The smoke was beginning to disperse; Munday's fuel had almost burned out. Kyle ran hard to the edge of the field, his eyes on the back gate. He could hear a continuous moaning, a long plaintive note of agony.

He approached the gate cautiously. One of Carlotto's men was lying on his back, his leg twisted at an impossible angle. Kyle moved in closer, but the man barely acknowledged his arrival as he reentered the garden. Kyle wasn't surprised – if his own ankle had been almost severed by a gin trap he doubted whether he'd be paying much attention to what was going on around him either; which was probably just as well because the guy was still preoccupied when Kyle encircled his neck with his arm and twisted hard.

He retrieved the dead man's automatic and ducked out of

sight beneath the kitchen window, still open from his earlier exit. He kept close to the wall, straightened up slowly.

It was quiet.

Way too quiet.

He sidled along to the window, slipped another cartridge into the shotgun, took a breath and cautiously raised his head up above the edge.

There was no one in the kitchen.

And it was still deathly quiet.

Kyle hauled himself through the gap as soundlessly as he could, clambered over the sink and crept to the connecting door.

'You can come in, Mr Kyle.'

The Italian's voice was smooth, untroubled. 'And I would prefer the shotgun to be broken, if you please.'

Kyle broke the gun, stepped into Carlotto's line of sight. To his right, Bates was still in position by the damaged window. There was a body slumped over the frame, arms hanging limp. Bates was still clutching the poker, the end of which was matted with hair and blood.

Nicely done, Bates...

Munday was slumped in the armchair and his daughter was standing over him pressing a blood-soaked handkerchief to his bicep. His pistol was lying on the floor beside him. The man Kyle had observed in the hotel foyer was at Bec's side, a thin stiletto pressed against the soft flesh of her neck. The man was dapper, his clothing more suited for a business meeting than a set-to in a half-derelict house.

'Cartridges out, please. And throw them to me.' As he waited for his request to be carried out the Italian began to sing: *Una furtiva lacrima ... negli occhi suoi spuntò ...*

Kyle did as he was told.

Carlotto broke off from his operatic rendition, bent and scooped up the ammunition. 'We are both reasonable men, Mr Kyle. I am here solely to collect what is due to me from Mr Munday following the regrettable termination of our business agreement.'

'It's not your money, Carlotto,' Munday hissed through gritted teeth. 'It never was. Your claim is invalid.'

'Ah, but that is where we disagree.'

Kyle glanced outside. The trench fires were still smouldering, the wind blowing the smoke westward and away from the cottage.

'Put the shotgun on the floor, Mr Kyle, if you please.' Carlotto inclined his head by a degree. 'And you—' this to Bates, '—fill the kitchen sink. Put the cartridge box in the water.'

Bates glanced at Kyle. He nodded; Carlotto held the winning hand. For now.

Bates picked up the ammo box, went into the kitchen. They heard the tap running.

The stiletto pressed a little harder against Bec's neck. She flinched, drew away, but Carlotto pulled her closer.

'Let me see to my father,' she begged. 'He's bleeding.'

'He will not die. Not yet.' Carlotto seized her by the arm and now the stiletto hovered above her eye.

Kyle flexed his arms.

'Stay where you are, Mr Kyle,' Carlotto purred. 'Or the lovely Rebecca may find herself … in the dark.' He smiled thinly at his own joke. 'Now, Mr Munday, the location of the money, if you please.' Carlotto revealed his teeth in a wider smile of anticipation.

Munday glared.

'Please, I need to stop the bleeding.' Rebecca's voice was a tense whisper.

'I'm all right,' Munday insisted. 'It's a scratch.'

'The money,' Carlotto repeated. 'Or you all bleed.'

Kyle was thinking hard. The non-appearance of the last of Carlotto's thugs suggested that there had been only three. He wondered what had befallen the fourth man – but it didn't really matter. It meant that Carlotto was on his own, one against four. The Italian had a slim advantage with the stiletto, and Carlotto was a careful man so Kyle had to assume he'd also be carrying.

'The money,' Carlotto repeated.

'Under the bed. A suitcase.' Munday sounded resigned.

'*Molto bene*. We will fetch it together,' Carlotto whispered in Bec's ear.

Kyle watched helplessly as he dragged her across the floor and disappeared through the bedroom door.

Moments later they reappeared. '*Grazie mille*.' Carlotto bowed and shoved Bec towards the front door. She was carrying a brown leather suitcase stencilled with the initials KM.

Bec shot him a look, glanced at the suitcase.

It wasn't fear.

She was prompting, hinting at something.

The front door closed behind them and Bates immediately leaned over the window frame and retrieved the unconscious thug's machine gun. A Thompson – old but deadly. She passed it to Kyle. It felt light; he quickly checked the drum. Empty.

He went to the door. Carlotto and Bec were negotiating

the bridge over the stream, the stiletto still pressed to her neck.

'Don't try to follow, Mr Kyle,' Carlotto called behind him. 'Or she will die. I promise you that much.'

Kyle believed him.

At that moment Rebecca did something with her free hand; she reached down to flick the suitcase lock. The case flapped open, bank notes spilled out, blew in the breeze in a cloud of green and blue. Carlotto cursed, yanked her arm, but it was too late; the money was out and dispersing fast.

Carlotto let Rebecca go. She dropped to her haunches, and Kyle saw that something else had fallen from the suitcase. He took a step away from the cottage, and then he saw what Bec had picked up. A Baby Browning pistol; small, but deadly enough. Bec didn't hesitate. She levelled the Browning at the Italian and pulled the trigger.

Chapter Forty-Two

Carlotto had seen the danger. He twisted away as the Browning went off, but lost his footing and toppled into the stream. As he lay on his back, half-submerged, Bec took careful aim and fired again.

This time nothing happened. The chamber was empty. She threw the gun down in frustration.

Carlotto was on his feet now, waist deep in water, gathering the soaked bundles of banknotes and stuffing them into his pockets. Kyle took three steps and launched himself off the bridge just as Carlotto's hand went to his inside pocket. As the pistol came into view Kyle hit him with all his weight, knocked him backwards into the water. The pistol went off just as Kyle's head went under, deafening him.

Kyle dragged the Italian to the surface by his lapels, but the stiletto was still in Carlotto's left hand; it curved down in a vicious, stabbing motion. Kyle caught the Italian's wrist and twisted hard but Carlotto's grip was firm.

The steel inched towards Kyle's face. Water droplets studded the blade, transparent beads glinting in the weak sunlight. Kyle managed to get both hands around Carlotto's wrist, tried to counter the inexorable force the Italian was applying.

Inch by inch, the blade receded. He was eye-to-eye with the Italian. Carlotto's pupils were dilated, focused. The tendons on his neck stood out as the blade hovered between them, held by equal but opposing forces.

But Kyle was a six-foot two wing-forward, and, despite his long layoff, his biceps were as solid as iron bars. He gradually pushed the stiletto one inch away from him, then another, and then another until Carlotto realised that brute force wasn't going to do the job. In a sudden change of tactic he released the pressure, feinted to his left and smashed his forehead against Kyle's cheekbone.

Stars danced before Kyle's eyes and he pitched forward, stunned, into the rushing water. His head hit the bottom, but the freezing current instantly brought him round. Coughing and gagging his head broke the surface in time to see Carlotto's retreating figure making his way along the stream, gingerly stepping from rock to rock.

Kyle waded after him, pulled himself out of the water and onto the rocks that studded the stream as it meandered eastward to join the river.

Carlotto stopped, turned, pointed.

The pistol.

Kyle ducked. When he looked up again Carlotto was picking up the pace, gaining confidence as he negotiated the natural obstacles in the stream. The banks on either side grew higher as Kyle pursued the fleeing figure. A sudden wave of nausea swept over him, doubled him over; he was forced to stop. He grasped his knees, took a series of deep, lung-wracking breaths.

By the time he felt able to continue Carlotto had disappeared. Teeth chattering with cold, Kyle plunged on in pursuit. His soaking clothes were slowing him down. He chose his route carefully; the rocks were mossy and treacherous. He followed the natural curve of the stream until he caught sight of the Italian ten or so yards ahead. Carlotto had come to a halt, feet planted on a wide section of rock that bridged the two sides of the stream. Away to the left a thin plantation of trees screened the lane along which they had driven earlier. Presumably Carlotto's vehicle was nearby.

The Italian had decided to make a stand.

But did he have any ammunition left? The weapon looked to be a 9mm Beretta. A 9mm housed a 15-round magazine. Which meant that the Italian had *plenty* of bullets left.

As if reading his mind, Carlotto raised his right arm, waved the pistol, and then threw it onto the bank. With the same hand, he made a gesture.

Come.

Kyle went. He stepped carefully from rock to rock until he was facing Carlotto. The Italian lifted the stiletto in a second, wordless invitation.

There was a gap, maybe three feet, between himself and Carlotto. Kyle needed impetus, but he didn't have much space to create it. He moved to the edge of his rock, tensed his leg muscles and jumped. He skidded as he landed and fell awkwardly at the Italian's feet with a bone-jarring thump. Dazed and momentarily stunned, he was dimly aware that Carlotto was already moving towards him.

Kyle was face down on the rock. In his mind's eye he saw the stiletto descending. He rolled onto his back and used the only weapon still available to him – his legs. He lashed out, aiming for Carlotto's kneecaps but the Italian had spotted the danger and stepped swiftly out of range. Kyle's kick found only space as Carlotto feinted to his left then back again, trying to work around Kyle's last line of defence. The stiletto described a hypnotic pattern in the air; up, down, from side to side, searching for a way in.

Kyle rolled, first to his left, then to his right. Carlotto stabbed at his legs and missed. Kyle dummied left then pivoted on the fulcrum of his backside. The movement brought him within reach of Carlotto's legs … which also meant that the stiletto was now a good deal closer than Kyle wanted it.

He had one second, one chance.

He grabbed Carlotto's trouser cuffs and jerked them towards him. The Italian's feet went from under him and gravity did the rest; the back of Carlotto's skull struck a projecting rock with an audible crack and the contest was over.

Kyle struggled to his feet. He prodded his ribcage and grimaced. Badly bruised at the very least. Breathless, he bent over Carlotto's prone body. No need to check for a pulse; the position of the limbs, the pallor of the Italian's complexion and the rivulets of blood trickling along the rugged contours of the rock told him all he needed to know.

Kyle sank to his haunches, put his head between his knees and let the weariness wash through him. As the adrenaline leaked away he became aware that someone was standing on the opposite bank.

'Kyle?'

Bates' expression was all concern.

He raised his arm. That hurt, too. 'All fine.' He pulled himself cautiously to his feet. 'Nothing critical damaged.'

'What about–?' She pointed to Carlotto's prone body.

Kyle shook his head. He kicked Carlotto's leg, turned the

Italian's left foot sole up. 'City shoes. No outsole. Smooth as a baby's bum.' He pulled out a wet handkerchief, retrieved the stiletto, wrapped it and put it in his jacket pocket. 'No weapon, no suspicion. A sad walking accident.'

'We can't just *leave* him here.'

'We can take him further upstream, dump him closer to the town.'

Bates made a face. 'And those other ... men?'

'I noticed a cess pit at the rear of the cottage,' Kyle said. 'Can't think of anything better to be honest. You?'

He began to pick his way over the rocks to the bank. Bates extended her arm, helped him up. He caught sight of Carlotto's Beretta lying where the Italian had thrown it. 'Better take that with us while we're at it.'

Bates nodded, picked it up and held it by the trigger guard.

'I wouldn't worry about prints. I'll make it disappear – permanently. Here, I'll take it, if you like.' He held out his hand and Bates gave it to him.

'How's Munday?' He allowed her to lean into him as they made their way along the bank towards the bridge.

'All right, I think. Rebecca bandaged his arm. The bullet went straight through – under his bicep. It's a clean wound.'

Kyle nodded. 'Good.'

'So ... what now?'

'Now?' Kyle winced as his ribs shot him a fresh bolt of pain. 'Now I could do with some breakfast.'

Chapter Forty-Three

Kyle slept for a good deal of the return journey. The Flying Flea overheated near Bath and they had to stop for an hour to let the overworked engine cool down. As they set off again, Bates fell into an uncharacteristic silence. Hardly surprising, he supposed, given the events of the past few days.

It suited Kyle. He didn't feel much like talking anyway. He let his thoughts drift, and of course, Colin-in-his-head was first in the queue.

So now you know, old buddy. Thanks for seeing it through...

You know me, Col. Never let a loose end trip me up.

Or a smooth sole, for that matter.

Ha ha! Love it...

I know you do. I do it solely for your entertainment.

Enough! I might die laughing...

The die is already cast, and I lost

Now that's not funny.

Lighten up, Kyle. What's done is done...

I know. But that doesn't help much.

The help comes from within. Or, put more simply, it's down to you from now on.

Thank you, Doctor.

Just doing my job ... or a job that could have been mine ...

You wanted to study medicine? News to me.

I was tempted. But I wouldn't get to wear a uniform, so that was that.

You're having a laugh.

Always loved dressing up. It was a weakness.

Plain clothes must have been a disappointment when you transferred.

You should see what I wore at home…

Kyle laughed out loud.

'What?' Bates glanced at him, frowning. 'What's so funny?'

'Nothing. Just thinking.'

'How's your head?'

'On the Kyle scale, around a five point five today. Life is doable.'

Bates was silent for a moment, then, 'What *will* you do, Kyle?'

Kyle pursed his lips. 'Who knows? I expect something'll come up.'

'That's not much of a plan.'

'Don't you ever want to just wing it, see what happens?'

'Not really.' She changed gear, and the Flying Flea lurched forward as she overtook a lorry. 'Maybe it's a personality thing.'

'My advice is, give it a try. Loosen up, Bates.'

A pause, then, 'Jude.'

'Sorry. Jude. It's a nice name.' He looked at her. 'Really. I like it.'

'I'm not mad keen on it, to be honest. But I'm stuck with it. Like I'm stuck with lots of things.'

She switched on the car radio, an action Kyle interpreted as drawing the conversation to an end.

He closed his eyes and thought about what Munday had

asked him to do. It was a small thing, he supposed, and it wouldn't put him out to do it. It was an explanation for changed plans, and people deserved explanations, especially people who'd gone to a lot of trouble. He was pretty sure Jacqueline Gower fell into that category.

Kyle dozed, drifting in and out of consciousness. At one point he was awoken by a rousing verse and chorus from Cilla Black belting out her latest hit:

When you leave me
Say you'll see me again
For I know in my heart
We will not be apart
And I'll miss you 'til then
We'll be together now and forever
Come my way

Step inside love and stay

He half-opened his eyes and imagined he saw a single tear trickle down Bates' cheek. He wondered what she was thinking, why the sudden lapse into silent introspection.

Lulled by the regular beat of the engine he fell back into a state of semi-consciousness. A while later he briefly came to and looked for a sign to tell him where they were. The Flea had stopped at a set of lights and the road sign read: *Newbury 3m*, which meant they were on the old Bath road.

That gave him a couple of hours to figure out how to get her to open up.

He snapped awake again. It was dark; the car had stopped

and the engine was off. Worse still, the driver's seat was empty. Hell, how had he slept so soundly? His head felt sluggish, sticky, as though he'd taken sleeping tablets.

He sat up, looked out the window to get his bearings.

Oh, *no…*

They were outside the police station, Bates' home base. Now he saw the envelope on the dashboard. He snatched it, tore it open. A single sheet of paper.

I'm sorry, Kyle, but I can't live with this. I have to tell the truth. I made a choice, but it didn't sit well with me. I know I'm risking a lot. Maybe you're right and they'll take all circumstances into account. Maybe my colleagues will back me up. Maybe.

If not, I'm sorry. I just wanted to say I've enjoyed your company, even though it's been a bit of a roller-coaster. I'm glad you found out the truth, and I won't say a thing about Munday or Rebecca. That's a promise.

Be careful, won't you? You'll find something that's right for you, and someone who's right for you too, I'm sure.

Maybe I'll see you around. Not for a while, perhaps … but it helps me to think that we might meet again sometime.

Best wishes for everything,

J x

PS Can you look after the FF for me? Thanks.

Kyle bit his lip hard.

Damn. Damn. Damn.

He wanted to follow his first instinct, rush into the police station and plead her case but he knew it wouldn't do any good. She'd confessed, and the matter was now in the hands of the CPS, the law courts, the judge and jury. Months of legal wrangling would follow, and at the end of it all a probable custodial sentence. He'd told her that mitigating circumstances would be taken into account, but Kyle knew first-hand how things worked in the Met. The murder of a copper by one of their own, and a woman at that ... female officers had a hard enough time of it, but for one who had stepped this far out of line...

He let his head flop back on the seat, let out a long sigh. Traffic rumbled by, groups of youths jostled each other on the pavement, laughing and joking on their way to the pub or the flicks. Couples strode purposefully homeward, arm-in-arm, smiling and chatting to each other as they walked.

Life going on all around him.

The keys were in the ignition. He got out, walked around to the driver's door, squeezed himself in, pushed the seat back as far as it would go, and fired up the engine. The A40 reluctantly coughed into life. Kyle let the engine idle for a long, long time.

He had no idea where to go.

Chapter Forty-Four

Kyle moved forward with play, waiting for the ball to come down the line. The fly-half, Tony Mears, had possession. Kyle felt the adrenaline kick in as Mears swerved and passed the ball to the centre, John Ottmann, a skilful player who'd only been with the team a month or so. Ottmann side-stepped two opposition players, dummied, was clear of a third and fourth.

Kyle kept pace on his outside. The full-back and opposite scrum-half were closing on Ottmann; Kyle read the moment, caught the ball as Ottmann unselfishly one-armed it across to him. He tucked it securely under his arm and pelted for the corner flag. The full-back was the only threat, coming in low to try to sweep Kyle's feet from beneath him before he crossed the line but Kyle was ready. He handed the player off with his palm held rigidly out to his right, felt the slap as he connected with the full- back's forehead, and then he was over the line, touching the ball down without the need to make a dive for it.

He was immediately surrounded by team members, clapping him on the back, congratulating him on his score. Kyle acknowledged them with a grin and a heaving chest.

'Get yourself fit, lad,' the captain, Brian Hamilton, quipped. 'You might make us a few more.'

Kyle nodded. 'I intend to.'

As he made his way back to the halfway line he noticed someone standing slightly apart from the other spectators. A woman, dressed head to foot in black. He shielded his eyes against the low sunlight.

Bec?

She saw him looking, raised her arm.

Six weeks had passed since the Welsh episode, although to Kyle it seemed much longer, but Bec's presence here could mean only one thing: Munday was gone. The cancer had claimed him quickly, as he had predicted.

Five minutes later the final whistle went. Rebecca was waiting for him as he left the field.

'Hello, Kyle.'

'Hello yourself. I wasn't expecting—'

'What the *hell* do you think you're playing at?'

Kyle was taken aback. 'What? Well, rugby—'

'Are you completely out of your mind?'

'No, just borderline psychotic.'

Rebecca's face was pale with repressed anger. She compressed her lips, probably trapping words she might regret. Kyle waited for her to speak.

'I just don't believe you.' She shook her head. 'You *know* what the doctors have said. You *know* what they told you.'

'Yep.'

'So, why this?' She waved, took in the expanse of the rugby pitch.

'They were short of a winger. So, I thought—'

'You know what I'm saying.' She began to tap her foot. Kyle remembered the gesture from way back; it meant she was really mad at him.

From the corner of his eye Kyle could see the teams

heading for the changing rooms. He wanted to join them, celebrate the victory, maybe down a few beers after showering. But here was Bec, large as life and twice as angry.

'I know what you're saying. But I have to live. My body, my responsibility. My risk.'

'And what about the people who care about you? What about them?' The foot-tapping increased in tempo. 'What about how *they* feel? Watching you commit *suicide*?'

'Look, it's only dangerous if I get into a ruck, or maybe if I'm unlucky with a bad tackle.'

'It's *rugby*,' Rebecca insisted. 'It's dangerous. Rucking and tackling are all part of the game, right? I remember *that* much. Players end up under piles of bodies all the time.'

'Sure, but they've got to catch me first. And they usually don't. That's why I'm playing on the wing.'

'I give up.'

Kyle allowed himself a rueful smile. 'OK, I can take a rap on the knuckles. But I'm being careful, I really am.'

'That did *not* look careful.'

There was an awkward silence. Gales of masculine laughter floated from the changing rooms, blew away on the breeze.

'Bec … I know why you're here. I'm sorry.'

She looked at her feet. The tapping stopped. 'It was peaceful, in the end. He just went to sleep. Didn't wake up. I managed to get drugs from the hospital, but he didn't want them. Only a little, on the last day. He was a tough old sod.'

He placed a hand on her shoulder. 'Let me get changed. I'll buy you a drink.'

She shook her head. 'I'm not staying. I just wanted you to know.'

'Walk with me for a bit.'

'OK.'

They set off slowly along the touchline. A murder of crows had already commandeered the opposition team's crossbar, lined up expectantly as though awaiting their own referee. Kyle wanted to know how Bec had played the unexpected hand she'd been dealt, how she had explained her actions to the police.

'Dad had it all figured out.' She toed the touchline, stepping along its painted length, her movements elegant and effortless as always. 'I brought him to a house in Gidea Park, after…'

'I know it. He took me there, too.'

'Uh huh. So then it was just a case of reporting to the local station. I told them he'd forced me to assist his escape, that if I hadn't complied he would make Sven suffer. I told them he needed medical care, someone to help him. That was the glue that kept me with him until he passed. He had friends – friends who would act on his instructions if I'd decided to make a bid for freedom.'

'Clever.'

'Oh yes. He had it all sorted.'

'A dying man's desire to die a free man.'

'Exactly. They bought it. I put on a suitably dishevelled and distressed show for them – like someone who'd been abducted would – then led them to the house. That was the hardest part. I had to leave him there, in their hands.'

'But you spent time together. That's the important thing.'

'Yes. They have no way of making the family connection, I'm sure of that … and Wales never happened. I made sure we left no trace in the cottage.'

Kyle strayed onto the pitch, kicked a divot of turf over the touchline. 'Did you see the newspaper report – about Carlotto?'

'In the *Express*? Yes. Five lines or so, wasn't it? London businessman dies in tragic walking accident.'

Kyle nodded. 'It was pretty much the same – almost word for word – in the *Mail*.'

They passed the posts and the crows took to the air in a leathery flapping of wings. Kyle wanted to take Rebecca's hand and only resisted with a huge effort.

As they arrived at their original point of departure he said, 'You've had a rough time. Jörgensen must have been a shock, and then your father…'

She lifted her chin. 'I'll survive.' She looked at him pointedly. 'And you will, too. If you start behaving like a sensible adult.'

'That's a little harsh.'

She smiled. 'Is it?' Now she reached for his hand and took it. 'Look, Kyle, we can't go back. Not now. But promise me you'll at least look after yourself. Be responsible.'

He sucked his breath in. 'Hm. A big ask.'

She was looking at him in the old way, the way that used to light up his spirit. 'I'm sorry to hear about your friend, Bates. She seemed like a nice girl.'

'She may get off. We'll have to see.'

'I hope so. But either way, she'll need someone to lean on, Kyle. Make sure you're that person.'

A final squeeze of his hand and she turned away, walked briskly towards the car park.

The lads were singing now, unrepeatable lyrics. Boys being boys.

Kyle waited until Rebecca's car nosed out onto the main road and disappeared from view, then went to join them.

Enjoyed this?

The second book in the Cameron Kyle series, 'The Fragile Coast' is due for publication in 2025

Or why not try the *DCI Brendan Moran Series* from the same author

Black December

DCI Brendan Moran, world-weary veteran of 1970s Ireland, is recuperating from a near fatal car crash when a murder is reported at Charnford Abbey.

The abbot and his monks are strangely uncooperative, but when a visitor from the Vatican arrives and an ancient relic goes missing the truth behind Charnford's pact of silence threatens to expose not only the abbey's haunted secrets but also the spirits of Moran's own troubled past . . .

Black December is an atmospheric crime thriller that will keep you on the edge of your seat until the stunning climax. This is the first in the DCI Brendan Moran crime series, one of the new breed of top UK Detectives.

'...gripping, with a really intriguing plot.'

Creatures of Dust

An undercover detective goes missing and the body of a young man is found mutilated in a shop doorway. Is there a connection? Returning to work after a short convalescence, DCI Brendan Moran's suspicions are aroused when a senior officer insists on freezing Moran out and handling the investigation himself.

A second murder convinces Moran that a serial killer is on the loose but with only a few days to prove his point the disgruntled DCI can't afford to waste time. As temperatures hit the high twenties, tempers fray, and the investigation founders Moran finds himself coming back to the same question again and again: can he still trust his own judgement, or is he leading his team up a blind alley?

'...non-stop action and convoluted twists. Another brilliant read in the Brendan Moran series...'

Death Walks Behind You

DCI Brendan Moran's last minute break in the West Country proves anything but restful as he becomes embroiled in the mysterious disappearance of an American tourist. Does the village harbour some dark and dreadful secret? The brooding presence of the old manor house and the dysfunctional de Courcy family may hold the answer but Moran finds that the residents of Cernham have a rather unorthodox approach to the problem of dealing with outsiders...

...a pleasure to read – gripped from start to finish...'

The Irish Detective - digital box set

The first omnibus edition of the popular DCI Brendan Moran crime series. Contents includes the first, second and third in series, plus an exclusive CWA shortlisted short story 'Safe As Houses'...

Silent As The Dead

A call from an old friend whose wife has vanished from their home in Co.Kerry prompts DCI Brendan Moran to return to his Irish roots. The Gardai have drawn a blank; can Moran succeed where they have failed?

Moran's investigation leads him to a loner known locally as the Islander, who reveals that the woman's disappearance is connected to a diehard paramilitary with plans to hit a high profile target in the UK. Time is running out. Can Moran enlist the Islander's help, or does he have to face his deadliest foe alone?

'Superb storyline with plenty of twists and turns...'

Gone Too Soon

Moran is called to a burial in a local cemetery. But this is no ordinary interment; the body of a young woman, Michelle LaCroix, a rising star in the music world, is still warm, the grave unmarked. A recording reveals the reason for her suicide. Or does it?

Why would a young, successful singer take her own life? To unlock the answer, Moran must steer a course through his darkest investigation yet, as the clues lead to one shocking discovery after another…

'…*endlessly twisty – an explosive finish*…'

The Enemy Inside

DCI Brendan Moran's morning is interrupted when a suicidal ex-soldier threatens to jump from a multi-storey car park …

Moran soon regrets getting involved when an unexpected visitor turns up on his doorstep to confront him with what appears to be damning evidence of past misconduct. Can the Irish Detective clear his name, or must he come clean and face the consequences? One thing seems certain: by the time the night is over, his reputation may not be the only casualty…

'…*a cracking, fast-paced thriller.*'

When Stars Grow Dark

A fatal road traffic collision uncovers a bizarre murder when it transpires that an elderly passenger in one of the vehicles was dead before the accident. All indications point to the work of a serial killer – but with little forensic evidence, how can DCI Brendan Moran and his team run the killer to ground?

To add to Moran's problems, an unexpected discovery prompts the Irish Detective to undertake a dangerous and unscheduled journey to Rotterdam where he believes his former friend and MI5 agent, Samantha Grant, is being held.

Can Moran succeed in his rescue mission whilst juggling the heavy demands of his most perplexing murder investigation to date? *When Stars Grow Dark* is number seven in the popular DCI Brendan Moran crime series

'...another brilliant outing for the DCI. No red herrings, page fillers or unnecessary characters, just gripping story leading to an unexpected ending...'

The Cold Light of Death

July, 1976 – Thames Valley, UK. Long, scorching days of blue skies, water shortages, and record temperatures. A newly promoted Detective-Sergeant is tasked with investigating the murder of a local shop owner – an investigation that goes tragically wrong...

Fast-forward forty-five years to 2021, when a chance discovery exposes a grim secret that forces a reexamination of the circumstances surrounding the ill-fated murder inquiry.

DCI Brendan Moran is assigned this coldest of cases, and it soon becomes apparent that he is dealing with a cold and calculating criminal mind. Can Moran and his team piece together the events of that long forgotten summer and unmask the killer before history repeats itself?

'A most satisfying read, with a plot zooming back to the mid 70s. As usual, wonderfully evocative. The entire series is a must for any crime fiction fan'

Closer to the Dead

A new cold case for DCI Brendan Moran coincides with the unexpected reappearance of a dangerous adversary.

As Moran grapples with an ever-changing work culture and begins to get to grips with the forty-year old murder of a young RAF aircraftswoman, an unexpected complication arises in his personal life that threatens to sabotage a promising relationship before it even begins. Could his new friend really be involved in the shady financial dealings of a cold case murder victim?

With this uncertainty playing on his mind, Moran throws himself into the new investigation, but as he digs deeper it becomes clear that the original case was sloppily handled, the interviews poorly conducted and critical evidence overlooked. Under the watchful eye of a newly-appointed Crime Investigations Manager, the team begin the painstaking process of tracing the original persons of interest.

Progress, however, is glacial, and so, when presented with proof that their progress is being monitored with alarming accuracy by someone who seems to always be one step ahead of the official investigation, Moran begins to wonder if he can make an arrest before the perpetrator falls into the hands of an antagonist with a very different idea of justice…

'Great story telling from a master of the crime thriller novel…'

In the Key of Death

The tranquility of a genteel household is shattered when an elderly piano teacher is found brutally murdered, leaving her sibling devastated and demanding answers. Enter DCI Brendan Moran, called out of retirement at short notice, to tackle the baffling case. As Moran delves deeper into the circumstances surrounding the murder, a web of complex connections and puzzling alibis among the suspects leave him struggling to pinpoint the elusive killer.

As the investigation intensifies, one of Moran's own team members becomes infatuated by the enigmatic leader of a self-sufficient commune, and suspicions are raised concerning a possible connection to the murder. With time running out, Moran must unravel the secrets concealed behind the commune's Utopian façade and navigate a dangerous labyrinth of deception to uncover the truth.

In the Key of Death intertwines themes of childhood trauma, psychological coercion and emotional manipulation – all wrapped up in a page-turning police procedural.

'...richly rewarding... Hunter spins a good tale...'

The Irish Detective 2 digital box set

The second omnibus edition of the popular DCI Brendan Moran crime series by CWA shortlisted author, Scott Hunter. Contents includes the fourth, fifth and sixth in series, plus an exclusive short story 'Inside Job'...

A Crime For All Seasons (short stories) - FREE via website

From the midwinter snowdrifts of an ancient Roman villa to a summer stakeout at an exclusive art gallery, join DCI Brendan Moran and his team for the first volume of criminally cunning short stories in which the world-weary yet engaging Irish detective reaffirms that there is indeed a crime for all seasons...

'...great characters, plot lines and dialogue. More please!'

For more information – www.scott-hunter.net

Printed in Dunstable, United Kingdom

64914273R00139